Christm

Yes, it is——

All our stories this special month involve
children at Christmas time, as the adults in their
lives try their very best to make the festive season
as happy as possible for the little, and not so
little, ones concerned, while finding their own
special person to love. And sometimes the kids
work a little magic of their own, for the best
present of all is to become a family.

Our four authors bring you their family traditions
from around the world. We visit America with
Jessica Matthews, Australia with Meredith
Webber, South Africa with Elisabeth Scott and
England with Caroline Anderson. The different
types of weather in these countries make no
difference to the warmth of the Season's
Greeting we send to you.

Dear Reader

I'm sure that, like me, you're already feeling that tingling glow that the magic of Christmas never fails to bring. And it's a magic that somehow binds together all the memories of Christmases of yesterday with the joy of Christmas today. Each Christmas, I find myself remembering Christmases when my sister and I were children—wartime Britain, but somehow our parents managed to find the magic for us. Broken dolls from a neighbour's attic, mended by our father—orange-box wardrobes filled with dolls' clothes our mother had made.

Years later, when our children were small and we didn't have much money, my husband and I did the same, although we did manage to buy the dolls. The joy on our daughters' faces is something I'll always remember. These three little girls, and their brother, are grown-up now, and passing on some of our family traditions to our grandchildren.

Christmas mornings are different for us now, but there is still the joy on small faces when they see the Christmas tree, and the excitement as the pile of presents under the tree grows. And the noisy, warm happiness of the family Christmas meal! Have a wonderful, magic Christmas!

Elizabeth Scott

HAPPY CHRISTMAS, DOCTOR DEAR

BY

ELISABETH SCOTT

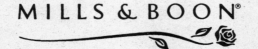

MILLS & BOON®

*MILLS & BOON and MILLS & BOON with the Rose Device
are registered trademarks of the publisher.*

*First published in Great Britain 1997
Harlequin Mills & Boon Limited,
Eton House, 18-24 Paradise Road, Richmond, Surrey TW9 1SR*

© Elisabeth Scott 1997

ISBN 0 263 80515 8

*Set in Times 10 on 10½ pt. by
Rowland Phototypesetting Limited
Bury St Edmunds, Suffolk*

03-9712-52107-D

*Printed and bound in Great Britain
by Mackays of Chatham PLC, Chatham*

CHAPTER ONE

'SPARE parts,' Matt said, and he took the list from Lesley's hand and wrote on it.

'Spare parts for what?' Lesley asked.

'For everything,' Matt said expansively. 'If we're driving through Africa in a Land Rover we've got to be prepared for any emergency.'

Lesley looked at him.

'You're not getting cold feet, are you?' he asked.

She shook her head.

'No, but I'm reminding myself that you're a doctor, not a mechanic, and I'm a nurse, not an assistant mechanic.'

Matt put the list down, and took both her hands in his.

'We'll learn,' he assured her. 'And it will be fun.'

It would certainly be fun, she knew that. Anything she and Matt did together was fun, and it had been right from the start. And this adventure, driving through Africa in a Land Rover, was going to be the greatest fun of all.

'Let's have another look at the map,' Lesley said. 'I want to see just where your brother's place is, see just how far down the map we have to go before we reach hot baths and washing machines and proper beds.'

Some of the names were familiar and some were very strange indeed, she thought as she looked at the map of Africa. Libya—Chad—Sudan—Ethiopia—Tanzania—Mozambique—

'I haven't even come to South Africa yet,' she said, peering at the page. 'And this Transkei—where is it?'

Matt pointed to a part almost, Lesley thought, at the bottom of Africa.

'It's part of South Africa—just a small part. Some-

5

where about there,' he told her. 'And you won't find
Thabanvaba Mission Hospital on it—we'll have to get
some large-scale maps. I'll get Peter to send us some.'

'It will take us ages to get there,' Lesley said.

'Of course it will,' Matt agreed. 'But think of the
things we'll see on the way. The pyramids—maybe the
source of the Nile—Kilimanjaro— We really should
take a side-trip to Zimbabwe—it would be ridiculous
to be so close and not see the Victoria Falls.'

Lesley sat back on her heels.

'A pretty long side-trip.' She looked at the map again.
'But—I had an uncle who went to see the Victoria
Falls,' she said slowly, remembering. 'He was working
in what was then Salisbury, and he went to the Falls. I
wasn't very old when he came home on holiday, but I
remember him talking about walking through the rain
forest early in the morning and coming on the Falls.
I've always wanted to go there since then. "The Smoke
that Thunders," the natives call them. Did you know
that, Matt?'

He shook his head.

'No, but I like the sound of it,' he said. And then,
exuberantly, he said, 'Oh, Lesley, there are so many
things we'll do, places we'll see. I can hardly wait.'

'But we have to wait a few months more,' Lesley
reminded him sensibly. 'We have that target we set,
and we've got to reach it, Matt, because we can't be
sure of finding work as we go.'

'I know,' Matt agreed. He covered her hand with
his. 'I'm not really unrealistic about this, Lesley. Jim
Foster—you know, the Australian guy in Paediatrics—
is arranging for me to meet a fellow he knows who has
done the whole Cape-to-Cairo thing—well, Cairo to
Cape—and he'll give us the lowdown. As we know,
there are only a couple of recognised routes over the
desert, and this fellow did all the homework before his
own trip so we'll be able to learn plenty from him.'

He shook his head.

'It's ironic, though. Doctors and nurses are so badly needed in so many of these countries but I believe the red tape is unreal so—yes, we have to save a bit more to keep us going until we reach Thabanvaba. And we're guaranteed jobs there. Peter says they're always desperate for staff, and he's already cleared that for us.'

'I like your brother,' Lesley said. 'I'm sorry he didn't have Clare and the children with him when he came to London last year.' She looked at the dark-haired man beside her consideringly. 'You're very like each other, Matt, but of course you know that.'

'Only to look at,' Matt returned. 'Peter was respectably married before he was my age and, look at me, you won't consider making an honest man of me!'

Lesley closed the atlas.

'You'd run a mile if I even suggested that,' she said equably. 'You must remember telling me, soon after we met, that you weren't the marrying kind.'

'Of course I remember,' Matt replied. 'And I remember what you said—that that suited you very nicely because you weren't either.'

He stood up and pulled Lesley to her feet.

'You don't have to hurry back, do you?' he said, keeping her hands in his. 'I thought we'd go to that new Italian place and have some pasta—cheap, you see, because we're saving—and a nice bottle of red wine, and then we'd come back here and—'

'I like the sound of that,' Lesley said, and although she was laughing she meant it. 'But I really do have to get back, Matt. Brenda has her midder exams next week, and I promised I'd go through some old papers with her.'

'Foiled again,' Matt said, shaking his head. 'I don't know why you won't just agree to move in here with me. It would be much simpler for everyone.'

'I know that,' Lesley agreed. She stood on tiptoe and kissed him, moving away adroitly when he would have caught her and held her closer. 'Don't you think we're going to have more than enough togetherness when we get going with this Land Rover?'

'Possibly,' Matt agreed. 'And we're probably going to be so hot and tired and dusty most of the time that we won't feel very romantic.'

Lesley looked at him, surprised.

'But we don't ever feel very romantic,' she pointed out. 'That's why it all works so well for us.'

Matt ran his hand through his thick dark hair.

'You mean the earth doesn't move for you, and here I was thinking I was the world's greatest lover!'

Lesley burst out laughing.

'Matt, last weekend we were camping, and if the earth moved it was because the guyropes weren't very well anchored!'

She lifted her coat from the couch and slung it over her shoulders, pausing at the mirror beside the door to run her hands through her short fair hair to tidy it.

'I'll keep the list,' Matt said, 'and if I think of anything else— Damn!'

The bleeper in his pocket sounded imperiously, and he reached for the phone. Lesley watched as he replied, intrigued as always by the change in him. The sleepy teasing in his dark eyes was gone, and the lines of his lean brown face tautened as he listened and gave terse replies.

'No, I was right here. Sure, I'll be there in ten minutes. And thanks, Kent.'

He put the phone down.

'Emergency appendectomy,' he said. 'And a hiatus hernia that looks as if it might rupture so we're going to do it at the same time. I assisted with one a couple of weeks ago, remember—Kent says I can do this one on my own.'

He grabbed his own parka and his car keys.

'I'll drop you off on the way,' he said. 'Save you getting the bus.'

His car was small and old and unreliable but fortunately it behaved impeccably now, and a few minutes later Lesley got out at the corner opposite her flat in the nurses' home and watched as Matt drove on through the hospital gates.

Brenda, her flatmate, was sitting on the floor beside the gas fire, her copy of Maggie Myles, the midwives' bible, beside her.

'Toxaemia of pregnancy,' she said briskly when Lesley went in. 'The symptoms are very like those of nephritis. Accumulation of water in the tissues, first noticed as swelling of the ankles.'

Lesley hung her coat on the book, and sat down beside her friend.

'Loss of protein in the urine and high blood pressure,' she prompted her. 'How're you doing?'

Brenda sighed.

'I know it all, I know I do,' she said mournfully. 'But I get this panicky feeling when I have to produce it for an exam.'

She uncoiled herself.

'I need a break, anyway,' she said. 'Kettle's boiling—coffee?'

A few minutes later she carried two steaming mugs of coffee back to the fire.

'I feel bad, taking you away from Matt,' she said. 'I shouldn't need support on this. I should just put my head down and keep it down!'

Brenda was small and red-haired, and she looked so unexpectedly fierce when she said this that Lesley had to laugh.

'Matt's off for an emergency op anyway,' she said. 'Kent Raymond is letting him do an appendectomy and a hernia at the same time so he's clearly more excited about that than about me not staying!'

Brenda stirred her coffee.

'I can't make you two out,' she said. 'You've been going around together for—what—must be over two years now. And for most of that time you've been considerably more than "just good friends". Now you're planning this trip through Africa, and you're going to be together day and night for at least a year. Am I right?'

'Probably more,' Lesley agreed cheerfully, 'because we're likely to be so broke by the time we reach Matt's brother that we'll have to stay there for a bit working and recouping our finances.'

Brenda tilted her red head.

'So is this a make or break thing?' she asked. 'Do you have to find out if you can stand being together as much as you will be before you think of any further commitment?'

Lesley put her mug down.

'It isn't like that at all,' she said, a little surprised that it should seem like that to Brenda. 'You say we're "more than just good friends", Brenda. Sure, we are— but that isn't the most important thing. We enjoy being together, Matt and I, but there's never been any question of further commitment. Neither of us has the slightest desire to get married at this stage.

'And, anyway, I'm not too sure that I would want to marry Matt when I do reach the stage of my life when I might think about that sort of thing. We're very fond of each other. We—all right, you can take that smile off your face, I know exactly what you're thinking— yes, we get on well in every way. But commitment and marriage? No, we're not into that.'

Brenda shook her head.

'You're not getting any younger, you know,' she pointed out.

Lesley burst out laughing.

'Brenda, I'm twenty-eight and Matt is a year older. We're not exactly over the hill, and I don't intend to listen to a word from any biological clock for years! Now, tell me about eclampsia.'

Brenda closed her eyes, concentrating.

'Eclampsia can be fatal to both mother and child. If there is any threat of this hospital treatment is mandatory. The pregnancy may have to be terminated at short notice and intensive treatment necessary to prevent fits.'

She held out her hand for the textbook.

'Go and have your bath,' she said. 'We can have another session when you've finished.'

Textbook cases are all very well, Lesley thought the next day when she took over from Night Sister, but they only fall into place when you're face to face with them.

'So—what's our round-up?' she asked as Sister Booth gave her the ward charts. 'Two delivered last night, I see, and both mothers and babies doing well. Three in labour now, all in first stage.'

'And one of them,' Fran Booth pointed out, 'is twins. So—have a good day, Sister Grant.'

'Thanks, Sister Booth,' Lesley returned. 'What do you bet that all three go into second stage five minutes before teatime?'

But she was lucky. Only one mother, and not the one due to deliver twins, had to be taken to the delivery room, and that was half an hour before teatime.

'Should be a straightforward delivery,' she told her student nurse, 'so you can do it. How many more do you need?'

'Three, Sister,' the girl told her. 'And I've only got two weeks.'

'You're on Flying Squad next week, though,' Lesley said. 'That should give you your quota.'

They went into the delivery room together, and the nurse with young Mrs Blackett, their patient, turned to them with relief.

'Here's Sister now, Mrs Blackett,' she said. 'And Doctor's on his way. Can I go back to the ward, Sister?'

Lesley nodded, abstracted, as she began to examine her patient. The student nurse, already accustomed to working with her, must have seen something in her face and in the momentary stillness of her hands. But she knew better than to say anything which might alarm the young woman on the bed, although Lesley was all too conscious of the girl's blue eyes on her face.

'Well, Mrs Blackett, this active baby of yours has got himself turned round,' she said easily, as her rubber-gloved hand identified a small foot where a small head should have been.

'You mean it's breech, Sister?'

Lesley nodded.

'Breech, and in a hurry, too,' she said. She smiled at her patient. 'But you do what I tell you and you'll be fine. Sorry, Nurse Roberts, I'll do this delivery.'

There was strong contraction and the young woman's damp forehead, her eyes dark with pain, made Lesley certain that this baby wasn't going to wait until Dr Mackenzie arrived.

'Don't bear down, Mrs Blackett,' she said. 'Remember your breathing—pant like a dog—that's it.'

When the contraction was over the student nurse, without needing to be told, wiped the girl's forehead.

'Has someone phoned your husband, Mrs Blackett?' Lesley asked, and her patient nodded.

'He'll be taking our Tim to his mother's,' she said. She tried to smile. 'He didn't want to be in on the birth anyway, Sister. Doesn't even like taking the dog to the vet's, he doesn't.'

Her eyes darkened with another contraction, this time too strong to fight.

'I can't—'

'It's all right, we'll do fine,' Lesley said.

One tiny foot appeared and then the other, and now the contractions were fast and intense and the mother couldn't help bearing down. Lesley managed to grasp the slippery little legs and began to ease the tiny body out as slowly as possible.

'Stop pushing now, Mrs Blackett,' she said, in a voice that her student nurse later told her no one would have dreamed of disobeying. Lesley turned the baby's shoulders, and suddenly she was holding a little girl, her small face red and outraged as she gave a loud yell.

'Good work, Sister,' Dr Mackenzie said from the door of the labour ward. 'Hardly worth my while to put gloves on—you've done it all. Any stitches needed?'

'None at all, Doctor,' Lesley said, and she couldn't help feeling proud of that for no breech delivery was easy.

The student nurse was beside her with a receiving blanket, and Lesley put the baby into it. A moment later the young mother was holding her new daughter.

'We said we didn't mind,' she said, touching the tiny face with one wondering finger, 'and we would have been just as pleased with another boy, but—oh, Sister, it's lovely to have my little girl!'

It was too late to go down to the canteen by the time Mrs Blackett was back in the ward, clean and fresh with her baby in a crib beside her, waiting for her husband to arrive. Lesley and Jane Roberts had a quick cup of coffee in the duty room instead.

'You know, Sister,' the girl said softly, 'I was looking at you when you delivered the baby, and—and you looked the way I felt when I did my first delivery. But you must have delivered so many babies.'

'Hundreds,' Lesley told her, not sure how accurate that was. 'But, yes, you're right, each time it's such an incredible thing. I can never get over how marvellous it is.'

The younger girl put her mug down on the table.

'I think I'll specialise in midder,' she said decisively.

'Get some good general experience first,' Lesley advised. 'I did a couple of years on a general ward first.'

'And you'll need that,' Jane Roberts said earnestly, 'when you and Dr Turner go off through Africa. You never know what you'll have to deal with.'

'Believe me,' Lesley said, meaning it, 'I could cope better with any medical emergency than I'll be able to if anything goes wrong with this Land Rover we're saving up for!'

*　　　*　　　*

Her times off duty somehow didn't coincide with Matt's over the next few days. They bumped into each other briefly once or twice in the canteen. Lesley told Matt about her breech delivery, and he told her about his appendectomy and his hernia. He told her, too, that in a couple of days he was to meet the young man who had done the Africa drive.

'We have to make it afternoon,' he said. 'Can you make it?'

Lesley shook her head.

'I'm on duty,' she told him. 'We can meet at night, though, so that you can tell me all about it.'

But two days later, when she came off duty, Matt was waiting for her.

It was raining, and he was standing at the opening to the passage that led from the hospital to the nurses' home. Through the windows Lesley could see the rain falling steadily, and she thought exasperatedly, Matt really is foolish, coming through rain like this with no raincoat. He's soaked. Whatever he has to tell me, it could have waited.

'Matt, for goodness' sake—' she began, and then she stopped.

Because there was something wrong. Something very wrong.

Matt was white, and his eyes were very dark. She had never, in all the time she had known him, seen him look like this. Her thoughts raced. He had been assisting in the theatre today. Had something gone wrong?

'What is it, Matt?' she said, not quite steadily.

He took both her hands in his. His own hands were icy-cold and wet from the rain.

'It's Peter,' he said, his voice tight, controlled.

'Peter? Your brother, Peter?' Lesley asked.

He nodded.

'There was a car accident. A landslide, after rain. I—haven't got all the details yet but—Peter is dead. And Clare.'

That far-off spot on the map, the mission hospital with the strange name. Distant, and unreal. But all at once too real because of this.

'Oh, Matt,' she said, unsteadily. 'I'm so sorry. So very sorry.'

Not caring whether any of the hurrying hospital staff could see them, she put her arms around him and held him close.

Saying nothing because there was nothing she could say right now.

There were practical things to be done, and Lesley was glad of that.

Back in Matt's flat, she put the gas fire on, made coffee and sent Matt to change out of his wet clothes.

But when they were sitting on the floor, as close as possible to the warmth of the fire, she said, as steadily as she could, 'The children, Matt. Were they with Peter and Clare? Are they—?'

He shook his head.

'No, they weren't in the car—they were back at the mission station. Peter—'

He stopped and then, very carefully, he started again.

'There was a call from the headman in one of the villages near them. His wife had had a fall, and they didn't want to risk moving her. She was eight months pregnant so Clare went too—she was a midwife. But of course you know that.'

Lesley put her hands over his.

'Yes,' she said quietly. 'I know that.'

He told her about the accident—the sudden storm, the landslide, the car skidding, the sheer drop. Now that he had started speaking he had to go on. Lesley could see that so she let him tell her all he knew.

And then, at last, he was quiet.

'At least it was quick,' he said tiredly. 'They both died immediately.'

Lesley hesitated, but only for a moment. 'How did

you hear?' she asked, knowing that Matt's and Peter's parents were dead.

'Clare's mother phoned to tell me,' he said. 'She lives in Cape Town, and she's there with the children now.'

Thank goodness for that, Lesley thought. Their grandmother was helping them to deal with this terrible loss.

'I suppose she'll take—' she began to say, but Matt's bleeper rang, startling them both. In a moment Matt was on his feet, lifting the telephone.

'Fractured femur? And Bob's gone off with flu? No, it's no problem. I'll be there right away.'

He put the phone down.

'Matt, you can't. You should have told Dr Gates about—about Peter. He would have understood,' Lesley said, standing up, too.

Matt was already pulling his jacket on. 'He needs someone, and I might as well get all the experience I can. You never know—' He stopped, and his eyes met hers.

'I have to go,' he said quietly. 'I'll give you a ring later. Do you want me to drop you off?'

Lesley shook her head. 'I'll give things a bit of a tidy,' she said. She managed to smile. 'Might even iron a couple of shirts for you, if I feel generous.'

At the door he turned.

'I don't know when I'll be back,' he said.

'I'll wait,' Lesley replied, and for a moment the bleakness left his eyes—the dark eyes she had never before seen with anything but laughter and warmth and teasing in them.

'Thanks, Lesley,' he said, and then the door closed, and he was gone.

Lesley took off her uniform and put on tracksuit trousers and a jersey of Matt's, rolling up the trouser legs and the sleeves. Then she washed the coffee-mugs and Matt's breakfast dishes. There were three shirts in his ironing cupboard and she ironed them, carefully, methodically, concentrating on what she was doing. And putting off, she knew, the moment of thinking about what this tragedy would mean to Matt and to her—beyond the loss to Matt of his brother.

In spite of the physical distance between them, they had been close—she knew that. She had seen the warmth and the affection between them on Peter's brief visit last year. Perhaps, she had thought at the time, listening to the brothers talking about their childhood in a village near Bath where their father had been the GP, the loss of their parents had drawn them even closer.

She put the shirts, still on hangers, in the small bedroom. There was a photograph on the shelf, and she picked it up. She had seen it so many times, but she looked at it now as if she were seeing it for the first time. The dark-haired man, so like Matt, his arm around his wife's shoulders. She was looking up at him, smiling, her shoulder-length brown hair tied back from her face. The little girl, Sarah, was very like her mother. She must be eight or nine now, Lesley thought. Colin, two years younger, was dark like his father, but he had his arm around the dog and his face was turned away. The baby, Jenny, was on her mother's knee.

Lesley didn't know she was crying until she had to wipe away a slow tear from her cheek. These people— unknown to her, apart from that brief meeting with Peter—this small, happy family. And the children, their mother and father so suddenly and so cruelly gone.

I'm glad their grandmother is with them, she thought again.

She made herself some tea and a toasted sandwich, and she phoned Brenda to tell her that she didn't know when she would be back. Then she lay down on the couch to wait for Matt. She must have fallen asleep, waking only when she heard Matt's key in the lock.

'How did it go?' she asked, sitting up and rubbing her eyes.

'All right,' he said, and he sat down and took his shoes off.

'Have you had anything to eat?' she asked him, knowing very well what the answer would be. 'I'll make you an omelette.'

He looked at her as she pushed up the sleeves of his jersey.

'Colour suits you, but you need to think again about the size,' he said, and he tried to smile.

'Oh, Matt,' Lesley said unsteadily, and she went to him, his arma reaching out to hold her close.

It was a long time before he let her go, and when he did she thought that it was a pity men found it difficult to show their emotions. My mother would say a good cry would help, she thought as she made an omelette and toast for Matt. And she's right.

'What's the world coming to?' Matt said as she put the tray on the small table. He smiled, but the smile didn't reach his eyes. 'You've washed my dishes, you've ironed my shirts and you've made an omelette for me. That's a lot of Brownie points for a liberated lady like you to chalk up!'

'Don't worry, I'm chalking it all up,' Lesley returned as lightly as she could because this seemed to be the way Matt wanted to deal with this.

While he ate they talked about the operation in which he had just assisted, but when he had finished he looked at her.

'You realise this changes things,' he said levelly.

Lesley nodded.

'Yes, I realise that,' she replied. 'There isn't much point in us going to Thabanvaba now. We'll have to think of somewhere else where we have a good chance of being able to work. My uncle might still know some-one in Zimbabwe. I could ask Mum to find out.'

Matt shook his head.

'That isn't what I mean,' he said.

She looked at him, not understanding.

'The children,' he said. 'Sarah and Colin and Jenny.'
Still Lesley didn't understand.

'Won't they go to Cape Town with their grand-
mother?' she asked. 'We'll get there sooner or later—
we can perhaps make it sooner than we would have
planned to—and we'll see them then.'

Matt's eyes were very dark, and his lean brown face
very still.

'When Peter was here last year,' he said quietly, 'we
had a good talk when I took him to the airport. I suppose
losing our folks when we were quite young made Peter
conscious of it, but—Lesley, he asked me if I would
take responsibility for the children if anything happened
to Clare and him. Oh, I don't think there's anything
strange—I don't think he had any premonition or anything. Peter is—Peter was always the careful kind,
thinking ahead. Making plans, just in case.'

Just in case.

'What about Clare's folks?' Lesley asked.

Matt shook his head.

'We talked about that. Clare's father has
Parkinson's—early stages yet, but of course he will
need more and more care. There's no way they could
take the children. Mrs Hulett can only stay at the mission hospital for a short time and then she'll have to
get back to Cape Town. She's terribly upset, but there
just isn't anything she can do. I told her it's my responsibility, and I will let her know.'

'What are you going to do?' Lesley asked, her
thoughts whirling. 'I believe the crèche at the hospital
is pretty good—Sister Hunt has her two-year-old and
her baby there. But. . .'

She looked around her at the tiny flat, which was
nothing more than a bachelor flat. No way could Matt
have three children living here.

'I have to do some thinking,' he said. 'I'll take you
home now.'

I don't really feel that he was shutting me out, Lesley

told herself later as she lay in bed, unable to sleep. This is his decision, and no one else can make it. But—but we're such good friends that I would have thought he might have talked it over with me.

Once again there were a few hectic and impossible days for both of them. There was a flu epidemic at the hospital, and every ward was short-staffed. Lesley had to do without her staff nurse on two days, and just when she came back the student nurse was off. She knew that they were under pressure in Theatre, too, and it didn't surprise her that it was three nights later before she and Matt could meet.

'Come and have something to eat as soon as you get off duty,' he said, meeting her in the canteen as she was hurrying out. 'I've got a frozen cottage pie to heat up. We have to talk.'

Yes, we do, Lesley thought soberly. We know each other so well, Matt and I, that I can't pretend that I'm not disappointed that we have to give up our dream— our 'African Dream'.

It was so selfish of her even to think that way, she told herself severely, when Matt had lost his brother, and these three children had lost their parents. And now that she had admitted to the thought, and brought it out into the open, that would be the end of it. All right, it was something they had both been dreaming of and planning for for so long, but it wasn't important when she thought of the children.

And of Matt.

Because, as well as losing his brother, he was going to have to face a complete change of life. She had more information about the hospital crèche for him but Sarah and Colin would have to go to school, and with Matt's demanding work schedule it would be unbelievably difficult to organise things. I'll help, she thought. I'll do what I can, but it's pretty much up to Matt himself.

And, for sure, he would have to find somewhere else to live.

'You'll have to move, of course, won't you?' she said that night as Matt put a plate of cottage pie and beans down in front of her and passed her a big bowl of salad.

It was a moment before he replied.

'Yes, I will,' he said carefully. And then added, 'Lesley, I'm going to Thabanvaba.'

'To bring the children back,' Lesley said unquestioningly. She had thought he'd have to do that—even if Clare's mother took them to Cape Town the long flight from there would be awful for three children on their own after what had happened to them.

'You won't be away for long, will you?' she asked.

Matt put down his fork and knife. His eyes were very dark and very steady as he looked at her.

'Yes, I will,' he said. 'Lesley, I'm going to take Peter's place at the mission hospital.' He leaned forward. 'I can't uproot these kids. Maybe later, but not right now. They're at least in familiar surroundings and there are people around they know well. Clare's mother says that even when she has to go back to Cape Town the folks at the hospital will manage to look after the children until I get there.'

He took both her hands in his.

'I've thought about it, and I just know it would be hell for the children to bring them here. Look at the weather. It's only October, and it's rained every day this week! They don't know anyone—they've lost their parents. The best thing I can do is see that some part of their lives doesn't change.'

There was a lot of sense in what he was saying, Lesley could see that. But to go from working in a huge city hospital, with all the benefits of modern science and with the constant back-up of experienced doctors and surgeons—

'You're taking on quite something, Matt,' she said.

He nodded.

'I know that,' he replied. 'But I know, too, that without Peter the mission hospital is pretty stuck. It isn't too easy to persuade doctors to go to a place like Thabanvaba, apparently. The back of beyond isn't in it—maybe to hell and gone is more honest.'

He poured another glass of wine for each of them.

'So—will you drink to my new "African Dream"?' he said. And then he went on, the laughter leaving his dark eyes, 'I daren't even let myself think about you and I having to give up our other African dream, I just have to keep on thinking that I have to do this.'

Lesley lifted her glass.

'Here's to your new African dream, Matt,' she said steadily. 'And you're right—you do have to do this.'

Matt put down his glass.

'Lesley,' he said, 'we always did mean to spend some time working at the mission hospital. They're desperately short of trained staff. Wouldn't you—?'

He stopped, and Lesley thought afterwards that he must have seen her immediate answer on her face.

She shook her head.

'No, Matt,' she said with certainty. 'That was different—that was short term and part of our holiday. I'm not prepared to take a big step like that. I'm—sorry.'

'Oh, well,' Matt said, and the lightness of his voice didn't succeed in hiding the disappointment in his eyes, 'it was worth trying.'

'Tell me about your plans,' Lesley said. 'When are you going?'

As soon as possible, he told her. There was, of course, red tape, but he had been in touch with the South African embassy and he had talked to the surgeons and doctors he worked with here, and it looked as if people were more than prepared to be helpful, recognising that this was an emergency.

'And the children, in the meantime?' Lesley asked.

Clare's mother would stay as long as she could—

her husband was in as a short-term patient in a geriatric
hospital where there were other Parkinson's patients—
and when she had to go the staff at the mission hospital
would look after the children, Matt said.

'Someone will move into the house, and the village
school Sarah and Colin go to is right there so that will
work, but the sooner I can get there the better.'

Already, Lesley found herself thinking in the next
days and weeks, Matt had changed. Oh, the old carefree
and happy-go-lucky Matt was still there, but the new
responsibilities, the new plans, had somehow made that
Matt difficult to find.

And no wonder, she would keep reminding herself
soberly. How would I feel if something happened to
Greg or to Michael? If our family circle and closeness
was broken like that? If I was faced with my whole life
changing the way Matt's is changing?

There were so many arrangements to make, so many
people to see, that all too suddenly the waiting was
over, and it was time for him to go. Lesley went to
Heathrow with him to say goodbye.

'You will write, Matt?' she asked him again. 'I want
to know how things go at the hospital and, even more,
with the children.'

'I'll write,' he promised. He touched her cheek gently
with one finger. 'Thanks for the presents you've given
me for them.'

'They're only small things,' Lesley said. A book of
paper dolls for Sarah, a small car for Colin, a bath toy
for baby Jenny.

It was time for him to go through—to leave her.

His lips were warm on hers, and his arms held her
close to him.

'I'll miss you,' he said, not quite steadily.

'And I'll miss you,' Lesley said.

And that was true.

More true even than she had realised. Somehow the hospital seemed quiet—dull—without Matt.

The hospital, and her own life.

'All right, you don't feel like coming to this party tonight, but just tell me this,' Brenda said, a fortnight later, 'are you going to spend the rest of your life sitting at home on your own? I thought you and Matt had the sort of relationship with no strings to it.'

'We did—we do,' Lesley replied. 'And I certainly am free to go out, to meet other people, to go to parties. So is Matt—not that he'll find much in the way of social life at Thabanvaba! I just don't feel like coming out, Brenda. It's only the beginning of November but this rain really gets me down. It makes everything so grey and dull.'

She could see the rest of November—the rest of winter—stretching out ahead of her in the same grey and dull way. And Christmas. Last Christmas Matt had come home with her to her folks in Surrey, and it had been such fun. This Christmas—

The phone rang, breaking into her thoughts.

'Lesley?'

'Matt!' she said, her heart lifting at the sound of his voice, far away as it sounded. 'Thanks for your letter. I've written two. Don't know how long—'

'Lesley,' he broke in. 'This whole thing is tougher than I thought. The hospital—I've hardly any trained staff. The children—and Christmas coming next month—they're very good, they're very brave, specially Sarah, but it's not easy for them.'

Over the long miles between them she heard him draw in his breath.

'Won't you think again about coming here?' he said.

Lesley looked at the curtains, drawn against the cold and the rain of the November night. She thought of the hospital—with no quick meetings with Matt, no exchange of news and experiences—and she thought of the times off duty without Matt. And she thought of three children, with their world so shattered and Christmas just around the corner.

But it was a big step to take.

'No strings?' she said cautiously. 'No commitment in any way?'

'None at all,' Matt assured her, and even over the poor line she could hear the lift in his voice. 'If you don't like it you don't stay. And I have to be honest, nothing will be easy.

'We have a maternity ward with only one midwife, and she's about sixty. There are clinics every day, and there just isn't time to see everyone who needs medical attention. There are dramas—two days ago I had an old man brought in with an iron spike impaled in his chest. The children are asking me if it will still be Christmas without Mummy and Daddy. Even the dog gives me funny looks, as if he thinks he should know me but there's something different.'

In spite of everything, Lesley had to laugh.

'Are you trying to put me off?' she asked him.

'No,' he returned. 'But I have to be honest with you.'

There was a silence now, a long silence.

Lesley took a deep breath. 'All right, Matt,' she said. 'I'll come to Thabanvaba.'

CHAPTER TWO

LESLEY had made her decision, and there was no going back on it.

Thanks to the efforts of some Very Important People, who were dedicated to doing everything possible to help the new South Africa, work permits were signed, flights were arranged and agreements were made at the hospital.

There were a few frantic days of farewells—to her friends at the hospital, to her family—and she was grateful once again for her parents' brisk and practical approach, tempered by warm hugs and her mother's suspiciously bright eyes. There was some rushed shopping for lightweight uniforms, a check on necessary vaccinations, parting with unneccessary possessions and then, one cold and wet November day, she left London.

The next morning she landed in Durban, but there was hardly any time to take in anything more than the wonderful view of the sea and the beach and the city, as the plane came in over the bay, because she had to hurry to catch her flight to Umtata, the Transkei capital, in a small plane. A very small plane, Lesley thought, somewhat taken aback.

She had told herself more than once that she certainly couldn't expect Matt to be there to meet her but, in spite of that, she found her eyes raking the crowds for his tall figure. Then she saw a board with her name written on it, and as she made her way to the man holding it he moved towards her.

'I thought it must be you, from what Matt said. Hello, I'm Ken Fraser.'

Lesley took the outstretched hand. Ken Fraser

was tall, with thinning hair, glasses and a warm, welcoming smile.

'Matt just couldn't make it,' he said. 'Too much going on at the hospital. This your case, Lesley?'

He lifted her suitcase, and led the way out of the airport and towards a dusty Land Rover.

'A long drive, I'm afraid,' he said. 'We've got a Thermos and some sandwiches—we'll have to start right away.'

His blue eyes were kind.

'We're all desperately sorry about Peter and Clare,' he said quietly. 'You don't know what it's meant to us, Matt coming out to take Peter's place. And now you.'

There was a great deal Lesley wanted to know, but she could see that Ken Fraser wanted to get going. And I'll know it all soon enough, she told herself as she climbed up into the Land Rover.

The ground shimmered in the heat, and she was glad of her dark glasses. And glad of the thought of the shady cotton hats her mother had insisted on her bringing.

The Land Rover's engine was so noisy that it made conversation difficult, but Lesley was glad of the chance to look around her. It's so, so *different* from anything I've known or seen, she thought. There was rolling grassland, with very few trees or bushes, and when they were some distance away from the town she could see distant clustered settlements of thatched rondavels on the hillsides.

When they stopped to have coffee and sandwiches she was glad of the chance to stretch.

'I'm afraid our transport isn't too comfortable,' Ken Fraser said. And then added cheerfully, 'We're always short of funds at the mission, and somehow there are always more immediate needs. And as long as we can keep this old thing going—'

He patted the Land Rover's dusty bonnet affectionately.

'I always like to stop here,' he said, looking around. 'This is a superb view.'

Each of the rolling hills had a cluster of small, thatched round huts on it, and Lesley could see smoke rising from many of them.

'The doors all face east,' Ken said, 'because that's the side of the rising sun and all the good spirits.'

He poured more coffee and Lesley drank hers gratefully.

'Tell me about the mission,' she said, feeling remarkably comfortable with this man. 'What do you do there?'

'I'm actually in charge,' he said a little apologetically. 'Of the mission, that is, not the hospital. That's entirely under you medical people. I'm the resident padre—minister—whatever. Sylvia and I have been at Thabanvaba for six years now—the longest we've been anywhere.'

'Isn't it a very isolated life?' Lesley asked him. 'For your wife, I mean. I gather that Clare was nursing again, but. . .'

She hesitated, not wanting to ask what on earth a woman could find to do.

Ken Fraser put the mugs and the Thermos back into a tall woven basket.

'Sylvia teaches the small village school,' he said. 'And she does a lot of work with the women—teaching them weaving, teaching them about vegetable gardening—she's pretty busy.' He smiled. 'We're a team,' he said. 'I'm there to look after their souls, and Sylvia does a good job with their minds and their bodies!'

They had two teenage children at school in Durban, he told her as they got back into the Land Rover.

'How are Peter's and Clare's children?' Lesley asked then.

It was a moment before he replied.

'They were, of course, devastated,' he said quietly. 'We had them staying with us until Matt came. Jenny is too small to know anything other than that her mother and father weren't there. Sarah and Colin. . . Sarah is a quiet little girl, anyway, and she has become even quieter. Colin—well, Colin goes from being very naughty to looking at you with such bewilderment in his eyes that you just want to hug him.'

On the point of starting the engine, he looked at her, his blue eyes holding hers.

'I think they're better, all of them, since Matt arrived. They're back in their own house. Matt is trying very hard to give them some stability, and it's made a difference to them already.'

Sarah wondered, for a moment, why it hadn't been possible for the children to stay on with Ken and his wife. They did have children of their own, of course, and obviously led busy lives, but—well, it *was* asking a lot of people to fit three children who were no relatives into their home and lives.

The last hour of their journey took them into more isolated country, with fewer settlements on the rolling hills. And then the man at the wheel pointed ahead of them. There, in the distance, Lesley could see squat concrete buildings. The hospital. She didn't know what she had expected, but for a moment her heart sank. Then she saw the grasslands rising behind the uninspired buildings, and on the skyline there was another group of thatched rondavels. Functional, she told herself determinedly. As a hospital should be. And there must be a wonderful view from the top of that hill.

When their vehicle drew up in a dusty compound and they got out Lesley was pleased to find that, with the sun going down, some of the heat of the day had dissipated.

'That's Peter's—Matt's—house over there,' Ken Fraser said, and he pointed to a low building a little away from the hospital. To Lesley's surprise, the white-painted house was softened by brilliant creepers—purple, rose, white, golden.

'Clare did all that,' Ken said. 'She struggled at first,

but it's worth it. Bougainvillea—hibiscus—and there's
a magnificent frangipani at the front, too.'

He lifted her suitcase from the back of the
Land Rover.

'Your room is over there in the nurses' home,' he
told her, 'but Matt said to take you over to the house
first. He said he'd get there as soon as he could, but
the children will be there.'

Lesley followed him.

Suddenly this was all too real. Here she was, in a
place and a climate unlike anything she had ever known,
getting ready to meet three children who had so recently
lost their parents. And a man she had thought she knew
so well, but a man she was beginning to wonder if she
had ever known at all.

She lifted her chin.

You've made your choice and you'll stick with it,
she told herself severely. At least for long enough to
give Matt a hand here—at least until he gets on his feet
with this. Because the deal is no strings attached, no
commitment—with work or with anything else. No one
forced you to say you'd come so now that you're here
you'd better make the best of it!

It was the dog she saw first.

He was at the gate, his hackles rising in his golden
brown coat and his ears alert.

'Hello, boy,' Lesley said, and she dropped to her
knees and held out her hand to him, trying to remember
his name. 'It's Murray, isn't it?'

Slowly the plumed tail began to wag and the hackles
subsided. Ken pushed the gate open. Murray came to
Lesley, stiff-legged, and sniffed at her hand. Then, very
deliberately, he sat down and gravely offered her a paw.

'He likes you, he likes you!'

A small dark-haired boy came running down the steps
of the wide and shady verandah.

'Murray likes her,' he called back, and from the shade
a girl came out. She had thick brown hair, held back

from her face in an Alice band, and wide-set
brown eyes.

'Hello, Sarah,' Lesley said quietly. 'Hello, Colin. I'm
glad Murray likes me. I'm Lesley—Lesley Grant.'

For the first time she wondered just what Matt had
said about her to the children.

'Thank you for the paper dolls,' Sarah said. 'I've got
all their clothes cut out now.'

'Colin, what you say to the lady?'

The woman on the steps was large, and she was
frowning at Colin.

'Thank you for my car,' Colin said quickly. 'I was
just going to say it, Patience. I hadn't forgotten.' He
turned back to Lesley. 'It's the only Porsche I've got,
you know.'

The big woman bent down and scooped up the child
who had come running from behind her. Jenny—fair-
haired, blue-eyed and with a sunny smile.

'She too small to say thank you, Miss Lesley, but
every night in her bath she play with that duck,'
Patience said.

She put the little girl down at the foot of the steps,
and Lesley knelt in front of her.

'Hello, Jenny,' she said softly.

Jenny's smile had gone, and she was looking at
Lesley doubtfully.

'She thought you were Mummy,' Colin said matter-
of-factly. 'She thinks every lady is Mummy. Sometimes
she calls Sylvia Mummy. She's too little to know,
you see.'

Lesley hadn't expected to be pitchforked into anything like this right away. For the first time she realised
just how little she knew about small children. But some
instinct told her that she must not brush aside what
Colin had just said.

'To know what, Colin?' she asked carefully.

The little boy was scuffing his sandalled foot in the
dust of the garden path.

'To know that Mummy and Daddy are dead,' he said, still in that matter-of-fact voice. 'There was this crash, you see, and the car went right over the edge of the road, a long way down. A very long way down. They had to get a special rescue car with a forklift to get our car up.'

'Colin!' Sarah's voice was anxious. 'You mustn't keep talking about the accident,' she said to her small brother.

Colin scuffed his feet harder, sending small puffs of dust up.

'Why not?' he demanded. 'I wish I'd seen that forklift getting our car all the way up.'

'I'm sure you do,' Lesley said, keeping her voice casual. 'It must have been a pretty difficult job.'

Little Jenny was now smiling tentatively. Lesley stretched out her hand and the child came to her, putting her own chubby little hand into Lesley's.

What now? Lesley wondered, at a loss.

She didn't want to push things by lifting Jenny up in her arms so she settled for a quick hug.

The little girl's sunny smile returned, and she said something incomprehensible.

'What did she say?' Lesley asked.

Some of Sarah's anxiety had gone. 'She says she'll show you her blankie,' she said shyly.

'It's really a blanket,' Colin explained. 'She just says blankie 'cos she's a baby. She takes it everywhere with her. Come on, Lesley.'

He led the way up the steps to the wide and shady verandah.

Small Jenny had retrieved something from under one of the wicker seats, and she held it out to Lesley.

'It's a lovely blanket,' Lesley said politely, touching the rather grubby but obviously much-loved blanket.

'Sit down, Miss Lesley. I bring tea out here,' Patience said. At the door leading into the house she turned.

'You be good children, now,' she said. 'Sarah, you see everyone be good.'

Sarah nodded. 'It's all right, Patience,' she replied.

Like a little old lady, Lesley thought, and her heart went out to the solemn little girl.

'It'll be nice to have tea here on the verandah,' she said.

'It's a stoep,' Colin told her. And then went on, thinking about it, 'But sometimes people do say verandah, people what don't know.'

'Well, now that I do know I'll make sure I say stoep,' Lesley assured him.

'Lesson number one,' Matt said, from the garden.

'Uncle Matt!' Colin shouted, and he hurled himself down the steps and into Matt's arms.

Small Jenny, too, ran towards her uncle. Sarah stood still, but she was smiling. A shy smile, but still a smile.

'Lesley, love of my life, you don't know how good it is to see you!' Matt said, putting Colin down and coming to her. His arms were strong as he held her close to him, and for a moment his lips were warm on hers.

'Oh, Matt,' Lesley said, not quite steadily. 'I've missed you so much.'

She wasn't sure whether it was reaction after the long flight or after meeting the children that made Matt's presence so unbelievably welcome. Or perhaps it was the dear familiarity of his lips on hers, his arms around her.

What she did know was that she hadn't realised just how glad she would be to see him—to be with him.

'And I've missed you,' Matt said, with complete truth.

He had known that he would miss Lesley—miss the fun they had always had together, miss their talking about work. Miss the laughter in her grey eyes, the way she wrinkled her nose when she smiled, the way she ran her hand through her short fair curls.

But he was taken aback at the way he felt right now, seeing her with one arm around Jenny, talking to Colin, smiling at Sarah.

It's sheer relief, he told himself sensibly. I'm just so mighty glad to have someone to share things with me that of course I'm glad to see her. And she's my girl, after all. For the moment, anyway, he amended hastily in his thoughts.

Patience brought tea out then on a tray, and Lesley poured tea for herself and for him and orange juice from the big jug for the children.

'Sit down, Jenny,' Sarah said, and when the little girl obediently sat down on the brightly woven rug Sarah handed her a plastic beaker. 'She might spill, you see,' she explained, watching her small sister while she drank.

'More,' Jenny demanded, and she handed the beaker back to Sarah.

'More what, Jenny?' Sarah asked.

Jenny beamed. 'More juice,' she said clearly.

Sarah sighed. 'I meant you should say, "more, please",' she said.

'More please juice,' Jenny said obediently.

'More please tea,' Matt said, and he handed his empty cup to Lesley. She filled it up, as well as her own, and then she leaned forward.

'Tell me about the work,' she said. 'About the hospital.' She looked at the children. 'Or should that wait till later?' she said doubtfully.

Matt shook his head.

'They've grown up with the hospital as part of their lives,' he said, his voice low. Sarah, her orange juice and biscuit beside her, had taken out her school books. Colin had gone back to placing his cars on the big plastic mat he had set out, which had a road system printed on it. Jenny, her blanket in her hand, was sitting close to Lesley. Even Murray was lying down beside Colin, asleep, although there was a twitch of his tail whenever a car came too close to the house. 'And they know you've come here to work in the hospital, like their mother did.'

Across the table, he took her hand in his and turned it over. It was small brown hand, competent and practical.

'It's a small hospital, as you see,' he said, releasing her hand. 'We have a TB ward, a maternity ward and a general ward. We also have a small ward that sometimes has to be used as a psychiatric ward while we're waiting to get a patient to Umtata—to the big state hospital there. The maternity ward is always busy. You'll be in charge. You'll have prenatal clinics and you'll have postnatal clinics, and in between you'll be delivering babies and sending their mothers away with advice on contraception, which you'll pretty soon realise they won't take.'

Lesley was looking at him in astonishment, her grey eyes wide.

'And while you do that,' he said, knowing that he should have let her absorb this more gradually but knowing at the same time how desperately he needed to share all this with her, 'I'll be treating my TB patients, sending them home with medication and strict instructions to come back for regular check-ups and knowing that I'm not likely to see more than half of them again.'

Lesley's hand touched his for a moment.

'I can see you needed to let off steam, but you needn't think you're frightening me off! I bet some of the folks I have in my clinics will accept the advice on contraception, just like some of your TB patients will follow up on their treatment!'

Her chin rose in the well-remembered way, and although there was laughter in her eyes there was determination there, too.

'Now, tell me about the general ward,' she said briskly, and once again he was taken aback at his relief that she was here at Thabanvaba with him.

He waved his hand vaguely.

'You name it, we do it,' he told her. 'Well, we do what we can, and when we're stuck we have to get patients to Umtata—either by road or, if we're lucky and there's one available, by helicopter. You see—'

He stopped as a nurse hurried through the gate and along the path.

'Nurse Moletsi?' he said, and he stood up.

The young nurse was breathless.

'Doctor, there is an old man here from the village,' she told him. 'He got a fish-hook in his hand some days ago, and now the wound has gone bad. Very bad,' she added.

Lesley was standing up, too.

'I'll see him in the theatre,' Matt murmured, more to himself than to either Lesley or the young nurse. Then he turned to Lesley. 'I'm sorry to do this to you, Lesley, but I could use your help.'

'No time to get my uniforms out,' Lesley replied. 'Can you find me a theatre gown, Matt?'

He nodded. 'We'll go right over,' he said.

Sarah was busy writing in her school exercise book.

'Lesley and I have to see to a man in the hospital,' he said to her. 'We'll be as quick as we can. Will you ask Patience to bath Jenny and Colin—no, I know you can see to yourself—and I'll try to be back so that we can have supper together?'

The little girl nodded, her dark eyes—so like Clare's eyes, he thought, with an all-too-familiar pang—on his face.

'If you're too late will you come in and say goodnight, Uncle Matt?'

'Yes, I'll do that,' Matt promised. He watched as Lesley set Jenny down beside Sarah, and waved from the step. Colin, busy with his cars, just nodded.

'It's an incredible balancing act,' Matt said, as he and Lesley walked across the compound. 'I don't know how working mothers do it!'

At the hospital door Lesley paused and looked up at him, her grey eyes level.

'From what I've just seen, Matt,' she said, and he thought how seldom he had seen her so serious, 'I'd say you're doing a pretty good job on one side—now let's see how you do on the other!'

It was ridiculous, Matt told himself, to feel so pleased because Lesley thought he was doing a good job with the children. Ridiculous, but he couldn't deny that warm glow somewhere around his heart.

'Right,' he said, and he smiled down at her. She smiled back. He led the way along the corridor, and into the small changing room beside the theatre. 'I'll have a look at our patient while you change. See you in Theatre, Sister.'

'Certainly, Doctor,' Lesley returned.

Darnedest thing, Matt thought as he strode along the corridor to see his patient, how much better I feel about everything because Lesley is here.

Darnedest thing.

CHAPTER THREE

THEY had worked together, Lesley and Matt, in the huge and sophisticated London hospital—on the wards, in the emergency room and in Theatre—at the start of their friendship. But they had never worked together in conditions like this, Lesley thought as she pulled on a green theatre gown.

This tiny changing room for theatre staff was not much more than a cubicle. There was no anaesthetist so Matt would have to work using only a local.

'Sister?'

Matt's voice was brisk and professional, and Lesley answered in the same way as she joined him beside the operating table in the small theatre. Small, and very basic, she realised with one quick, appraising glance.

'Sorry to rush you into this,' Matt said, without looking up. 'We're so short-staffed on the wards that I can't ask anyone else to come. Now, Jacob has this fish-hook in his hand and we're going to take it out. You've been very foolish, Jacob, not coming to the hospital right away.'

'Sorry, Doctor,' the old man murmured. 'I think it will come out by itself, you see.'

He was drowsy, Lesley saw as she checked the prepared instruments. Although she hadn't worked in Theatre for some time, her training surfaced immediately.

'He's had a good shot of pethidine,' Matt said as she swabbed the old man's hand and wrapped a sterile towel around it. He scrubbed up himself and Lesley handed him gloves. By then the old man was almost asleep.

'Infection's spread to the lymphatic system,' Matt said, and he pointed to a thin red line running up Jacob's

38

the compound, lit now by overhead lights, to the house.

She went slowly to find her room. Of course Matt had to leave her here. Foolish to feel a little—abandoned, she told herself firmly. And foolish, too, to be disturbed by the coolness in Sister Botha's eyes.

One of the doors was open, and her suitcase was sitting in the middle of the floor with her airways bag beside it. Just along the corridor there was a bathroom, and she showered quickly and changed into a cotton dress. A little crumpled, she thought, looking at herself in the mirror, but what a relief to get out of the clothes she'd been travelling in.

It was a strange thought that the trousers and shirt were what she'd been wearing when she flew out of London. Just yesterday, she realised, but it seemed much longer ago. And half a world away. At least the rose-pink colour of the cotton dress did something for her face and her hair.

I'm very pale, she thought, remembering the dark-haired sister's suntanned face and brown arms. Matt, too, already looked different from the Matt who had left London.

The heat of the day had gone, but it was still very warm, as she hurried across to the doctor's house.

The children were out on the verandah—no, she reminded herself, the stoep—sitting on the swing seat, little Jenny in the middle. They were all bathed, the girls in rose-sprigged shortie cotton pyjamas and Colin in a miniature T-shirt and shorts with a large dinosaur rearing across his small chest.

'Uncle Matt is showering. He'll be ready soon,' Sarah said. 'We have to eat right away because it's late for Jenny. She's usually in bed by now.'

Little Jenny did look sleepy. Sleepy, and adorable, Lesley thought, with her fair curls fluffy, her cheeks pink and a dimple showing when she smiled at Lesley.

'I like your dinosaur,' Lesley said to Colin.

'He's a Tyrannosaurus rex,' the little boy told her.

'He's the fiercest of them all—he can kill any other dinosaur.'

'He certainly looks fierce,' Lesley agreed.

'I've got lots of books about dinosaurs,' Colin told her. 'I could let you see them, if you like. You prob'ly don't know very much about dinosaurs.'

'No, I don't,' Lesley agreed. 'Thank you, Colin, I'd like to see your dinosaur books.'

'I'll just get them,' Colin said, but his sister's hand on his arm restrained him.

'Not now, Colin. You know Uncle Matt said we had to have supper right now, and—'

'And everybody does what Uncle Matt says because he can be fiercer than a Tyrannosaurus rex!' Matt said, coming out of the front door. He had changed into a T-shirt and cotton trousers, and his thick dark hair was still wet. 'Thanks, Sarah, for keeping everything in order. We'll look at your books later, Colin. Patience is bringing supper out now. We eat outside in the evenings, Lesley—it's so nice and cool.'

Supper was meatballs in gravy with rice and vegetables, followed by pink pudding. Lesley looked at Matt across the table.

'Very nice,' she said gravely, meaning it.

'Very,' he agreed, and there was laughter in his dark eyes. 'I've become very fond of meatballs. And of pink pudding. When in Rome, you know.'

Sarah put her spoon down.

'You're not in Rome, Uncle Matt,' she said, perplexed.

'No, I'm not,' Matt agreed. 'But there's a saying, Sarah—when in Rome, do as the Romans do. Now, you and Colin and Jenny like meatballs and rice, and you like pink pudding, so—well, I'm enjoying them, too.'

Sarah thought about that.

'But it isn't what you usually eat,' she said.

'No, it isn't,' Matt agreed.

Jenny had succeeded in getting pink pudding over most of the high chair, as well as over most of her small self. Matt looked at her.

'Patience did say it wasn't a good idea to bath Jenny before supper,' he said ruefully.

'I'll clean her up,' Lesley said. 'Sarah, will you show me where the bathroom is?'

She lifted Jenny from the high chair, keeping as much of the pink pudding away from herself as possible, and followed Sarah through the hall. Thanks to the large plastic bib, the baby was easier to clean up than Lesley had thought.

'Most of the pink pudding is in the pocket of this bib,' she said, surprised.

'That's why the bib is made like that,' Sarah told her. 'To catch things babies spill. 'Cos babies do spill an awful lot.'

'That's very clever,' Lesley said, inspecting the now-clean bib with admiration.

'You don't know much about babies, do you?' Sarah asked, her brown head tilted to one side.

'No, I don't,' Lesley agreed. 'Neither babies nor dinosaurs.' She looked at Jenny. 'There you are, poppet, good as new. Let's see what Uncle Matt's orders are now.'

But it seemed that Uncle Matt's orders had already been given for Patience met them halfway along the hall.

'Time for Jenny to go to bed,' she said, her broad face creased in a smile as she took the baby from Lesley's arms. 'She just say goodnight to her uncle, then I put her to bed. Sometimes Dr Matt put her to bed, but he not so good yet with the nappies. But he learning!'

It was quite a picture, Lesley thought, Matt learning how to change nappies. But something else was quite a picture, and that was Matt taking little Jenny in his arms, cuddling her and then kissing her fair curls before he gave her back to Patience.

'What would I do without you, Patience?' he said, as she turned to go.

'You be in big trouble, Dr Matt,' Patience told him, and she smiled.

Bedtime for Sarah and Colin involved Matt more. Matt *and* herself because Colin insisted on showing her his dinosaur books and his dinosaur models, lined up side by side with some small knights in armour. Lesley felt more at home in Sarah's room, with dolls and small furry animals set out neatly.

'I like your room, Sarah,' she said, and she touched the rose-sprigged curtains. 'I used to have curtains something like this when I was just a little older than you.'

'Mummy made them,' Sarah told her, and Lesley was pretty sure that it needed quite an effort for the little girl to keep her voice steady. 'We went to Cape Town just after last Christmas to see Granny, and Mummy let me choose the material. She made the curtains as soon as we came home.'

'She made a lovely job of them,' Lesley said, touching the ruffled frill.

'Sarah, I heard you talking about Christmas.' Colin appeared in the doorway, his dark hair rumpled, a shabby teddy under one arm and a large green dinosaur under the other. 'What were you saying?' he asked, more than a little truculently.

'We were talking about my curtains and last Christmas,' Sarah said. 'Not this Christmas.' She sighed, as if the weight of all the world lay on her thin shoulders.

'Colin thinks Christmas isn't—isn't going to be very nice,' she said, and there was a wobble in her voice, 'without Mummy and Daddy.'

It was all too clear that not only Colin thought that

Christmas might not be very nice. Lesley felt as if there might be a wobble in her own voice.

'We'll have to think about Christmas, won't we?' she said as lightly as she could. 'I think if we all try we can make it—not too bad. But, yes, it's sad to think about Christmas without your mummy and daddy.'

She said goodnight to both children, peeped in on Jenny and went back outside to wait while Matt said goodnight to them.

It was quite a while before he came out and Lesley, sitting in the swing seat, felt her eyelids drooping.

'I heard the Christmas bit,' he said, sitting down beside her and taking her hand in his. 'You're right, we will have to think about it.'

'It's only five weeks away,' Lesley said. And then, before she could stop herself, she exclaimed, 'Oh, Matt, you really have taken on something!'

'I know that,' Matt replied. 'But I had to—I had promised Peter. I couldn't back out of that. And you know, Lesley, even in the short time I've been here I can see that things are getting better. Just being in their own house helped. And this stupid mutt here—Ken and Sylvia couldn't have him because they have cats and the kids missed him. Hey, Murray?'

Murray, lying at his feet, wagged his tail.

There was only a dim light now on the stoep, and the air was warm and fragrant with the smell of the creepers around them. The crescent moon was high in the cloudless sky, and Lesley found herself thinking that it was like a dream, the two of them here in this strange and unfamiliar place, when such a short time ago they had been in London, planning for their African dream.

She sat up.

'You know what, Matt?' she said. 'We talked about our African dream. Well, we had to give it up, but now we've got another African dream. Except—except it isn't a dream, it's real.'

'Very real,' Matt agreed. 'You're quite a girl. Lesley, taking this in your stride.'

'Wait a minute, now,' Lesley said quickly. 'Remember our deal—it's much too early for me to know whether I can take it in my stride. Give me a chance to see how things go.'

In the dim light she could see him looking down at her.

'I did say no strings attached, but will you at least give it until after Christmas?' he said very quietly. 'I don't think I could handle Christmas for them on my own.'

'I think I've already agreed to that,' Lesley said, and she thought of Sarah's brown eyes looking up at her when she'd said that Colin thought Christmas might not be very nice. And thought of Colin, his lower lip trembling just a little in spite of his truculence. And baby Jenny, asleep in her cot on her tummy with her well-padded little bottom in the air, her thumb in her mouth and her blanket held close to her.

'You must be tired, Lesley,' Matt said.

'I am,' Lesley replied. 'I didn't sleep much on the overnight flight, and it's been quite a day.'

He was very close to her in the warm darkness, and after everything that was so strange and so new the dear familiarity of his arms around her, of his lips on hers, was comforting.

And more than comforting, she realised with some surprise as the gentle warmth of Matt's lips on hers became more demanding and his arms tightened around her.

And then, suddenly, he let her go.

'I did say I'd missed you, didn't I?' he said, not quite steadily. 'I hadn't realised just how much.'

He stood up and took her hands, drawing her to her feet.

'I'm not that tired,' Lesley said, but he didn't reply as he led the way down the steps and along the garden path.

There was no one around, and only a few lights on in the squat hospital building.

'I don't suppose there are any rules about when you have to be in,' Matt said as they crossed the compound towards the hospital, 'but we'd better get you back.'

'There had better not be any rules,' Lesley returned. 'I'm not a student nurse, I'm a qualified Sister and perfectly able to make my own rules!'

In the darkness he looked down at her, and she was all at once very conscious, in a new and a strange way, of the nearness of his body to hers.

'Some of the rules—might have to be changed, Lesley,' he said.

For a moment she thought that he was going to say more than that, but then he put both hands on her shoulders and looked down at her. His lips brushed hers, and he murmured goodnight.

Slowly Lesley went along the corridor and into her room. She hadn't unpacked and she didn't intend to right now, but she laid out her uniform ready for the next day—carefully, methodically, as she always had done—and she set her small alarm clock.

All the other lights were out, she noticed as she came back from the bathroom, ready for bed in her cotton shortie pyjamas which fortunately had been near the top of her suitcase. She switched off her own light, realising that two nights ago she had slept in her own bed at home, last night she had been on the plane and now here she was in Thabanvaba.

But then, tired as she was, she lay with only the sheet over her, thinking about what Matt had said. 'Some of the rules might have to be changed.'

It was something she hadn't thought about—a change in their relationship. Their lovemaking, like the rest of their relationship, had been light-hearted and uncomplicated. It was part of their—friendship, their closeness. No more than that.

But now—

She could see the practical difficulties. She couldn't have gone with Matt to his room in the house, and he certainly couldn't have come here with her.

But there was more than that. Something had changed—the way Matt had held her, the way he had kissed her. There had been something new, something—disturbing in that kiss.

And she wasn't sure how she felt about that.

There were only six beds in the small maternity ward, but they were all occupied. Four of the young mothers had their babies in cots beside them, the other two hadn't delivered.

And, as Matt had said, the only other midwife, Sister Cekiso, around sixty. But she had packed a lot of experience in delivering babies into these years, Lesley realised pretty soon.

'Two of the babies were born yesterday, the other two last night,' she told Lesley matter-of-factly. 'Now that you are here, Sister Grant, I will go off duty.'

'You've been on duty all day and all night, too?' Lesley asked, taken aback.

The older sister shrugged.

'There was noone else to deliver the babies,' she said. 'Dr Matt was busy.' She smiled, her plump cheeks creasing. 'And I think, Sister Grant, that I have more experience with babies than Dr Matt does!'

'I'm sure you do,' Lesley agreed, already liking this woman.

Dr Matt, she thought. They seem to call him Dr Matt. I suppose, to all of them, Dr Turner meant Peter.

'Can we discuss duty times when you've caught up on sleep, Sister Cekiso?' she asked. And as she said it she thought, She's much older than me—she should be the senior sister. I'll have to check that out with Matt.

Sister Cekiso was sitting at the desk, filling in the charts. She looked up and smiled.

'Sister Grant,' she said pleasantly, 'I am not good

with the administration. I am only good at delivering babies! I will be happy to leave all the organising to you. You will find young Faith works well, but she is young, and she has to be told very clearly what to do.'

She stood up, and lifted her large handbag from the floor beside the desk.

'And now I will go to my room and sleep.'

She had a room in the nurses' home, she told Lesley, but the village she lived in was the one on the top of the hill behind the hospital so she went home as often as she could.

Lesley's first day flew past. Halfway through the morning one of the young mothers in labour delivered, a quick, straightforward delivery which meant that she wasn't worried about leaving the young nurse-aide, Faith Hlazo, in charge of the ward.

Faith, and Patience in charge of the children, she thought, and she wondered when Hope and Charity would appear. But of course this was a mission station.

Managing a large maternity ward at St Margaret's was very different from being in charge of this small ward here at Thabanvaba, she found herself thinking at odd moments through that first busy day. But, in spite of the differences, there was enough hospital routine for there to be a reassuring familiarity.

She had a quick lunch in the small staff dining-room, finding only Sister Botha there when she went in.

'Hello,' Lesley said, as she sat down opposite the dark-haired girl. 'Matt didn't say what your first name is—I'm Lesley.'

'Anna-Marie,' the other sister replied. Stiffly, Lesley thought, but she decided to ignore that.

'You're in charge of General—that must be quite a heavy load,' she said, helping herself to some cold chicken and salad.

'I can manage it. I trained at Groote Schuur,' the dark-haired girl replied, and now there was no doubt about the coolness in her voice.

'Heavens, I didn't mean you couldn't cope with it,' Lesley said, taken aback. 'I just meant it must be a lot of work.' There was no reply so she had one more try. 'Groote Schuur, that's in Cape town, isn't it? The one where the first heart transplant op was done.'

Anna-Marie Botha nodded.

'I have to get back to my ward,' she said dismissively, and she carried her plate and her cutlery to the serving-hatch. As she turned towards the door it opened and Matt came in, his white coat flying and his dark hair untidy.

'Hello, Anna-Marie,' he said. 'Lesley, you've survived the morning, at least. How did it go?'

'Fine—I think,' Lesley replied, very glad to see him. And realised later that it probably showed very clearly on her face.

'Couldn't be worse than that first morning we were both on Casualty,' Matt said cheerfully. 'Remember the chaos? There had been a bus accident, and people were being brought in in hundreds.'

'And in the middle of it the old man who had cut his foot went into cardiac arrest,' Lesley said.

'I thought I would go into cardiac arrest myself.'

His plate piled full, he sat down beside Lesley. And Lesley, turning towards him, saw for a moment cool hostility on Anna-Marie Botha's face before she turned and went out of the dining-room.

'At least you've got to know the only other English-speaking member of the staff, besides you and me,' Matt said.

'English-speaking, yes,' Lesley said, thinking about that. 'But somehow the way she speaks—very carefully—and something about her accent—what is it that's different?'

'Not surprising,' Matt returned. 'She's Afrikaans. She'd be much more comfortable using that so I do use English-speaking loosely!'

'And the rest of the staff—Sister Cekiso speaks

English, and so does Faith,' Lesley said. 'But you're right, it's obviously not their home language.'

'Oh, yes, they do all speak English, but their home language is Xhosa—the tribal language around here.'

'Xhosa.' Lesley tried the word out.

Matt shook his head.

'I don't say it properly either,' he said. 'There's a sort of a click on the first two letters—ask Agnes Moletsi to say it for you.'

Lesley finished her coffee and without asking, carried some over for Matt.

'I must get back to my ward,' she said. 'I think I'll have the other delivery pretty soon.'

'I'll look in later if I can—thanks,' Matt said, taking the coffee-cup from her. 'I'm afraid we don't go in for regular doctors' rounds here—there just isn't time— but if you need me send for me.'

Lesley was back in her ward just in time to deliver the other baby, and later that afternoon a young black man appeared at the door of the ward, looking anxious.

'My wife is coming to have baby,' he said.

'Bring her in, then,' Lesley said, working out in her mind that the new patient would have to sleep in the delivery room because all six beds in the ward were occupied. 'How close are her contractions?'

He looked at her blankly.

'Is the baby coming soon?' she asked carefully. To her surprise, his face lit up and a torrent of words burst out.

'Faith, I need you,' Lesley called. When the young nurse-aide came she said, 'Just ask him how close the contractions are, and then tell him to bring her in—I suppose she's outside.'

She listened, fascinated, at the conversation between Faith and the young man, and then Faith turned to her, smiling.

'The baby is born already. He is with his mother outside,' she said. 'That is what he is telling you.'

'BBA,' Lesley murmured five minutes later, as she held a tiny but obviously vocal little boy, and expertly clamped the umbilical cord.

'What is that you are saying?' Faith asked, looking up from cleaning up the young mother.

'Born Before Arrival,' Lesley told her. 'It happens even in big hospitals—I'd guess it can happen even more often here.'

But the baby was fine and so was the mother—and so was the young father after he had been given a cup of strong sweet tea.

'Will tomorrow be quieter, do you think?' Lesley asked, as Faith was leaving.

'Oh, no, Sister,' the girl replied seriously. 'It will be much more busy because tomorrow we have clinic.'

Sister Cekiso appeared then, looking rested, and Lesley brought her up to date with the ward and handed over the charts. The older woman was happy, she said, to do night duty at the moment and leave Lesley on days.

'But you can't work every night, and I'll need time off, too,' Lesley said. 'I'll see what Dr Turner can suggest.'

Some of the heat of the day had gone and, although she was tired, instead of going to her room she walked across the dusty compound to the gate to the doctor's house. Matt was still busy—she had seen his tall figure moving around the general ward—but she wanted to see the children, even if only briefly. Because doing what she could to help with the children was part of her reason for being here, and she wasn't prepared to let the undoubted pressures of working in this understaffed hospital make her forget that.

'Hi, Lesley,' Colin said, as casually as if he had known her for years, when she opened the gate and walked up the path. He was flat on his stomach on the stoep floor, industriously building with Lego.

'What are you making?' Lesley asked.

'A space-station,' he told her, without looking up. 'But I'm making a garage for that Porsche you gave me. The captain of the spaceship likes to bring his own car with him when he goes to other planets.'

'Yes, I'm sure he does,' Lesley agreed.

'Hello, Lesley—I'm Sylvia. I looked into your ward earlier, but you were much too busy to be disturbed.'

Sylvia Fraser's brown hair was tied back from her face. She had blue eyes and a warm smile, and the clasp of her hand was firm.

'I've been hearing Sarah's homework,' she said. 'It saves Matt some time later.'

Sarah, sitting beside her at the table, looked up and smiled shyly.

'I'm almost finished,' she said, 'and then I'm going to play with my paper dolls. I forgot to let you see them all cut out last night.'

'I'll see them as soon as you've finished,' Lesley said. 'Where's Jenny?'

'She's with Patience in the kitchen,' Sylvia said. She looked down at Sarah's brown bent head. And then, casually, she moved a little distance away, taking Lesley with her.

'Patience is an absolute blessing,' she said, her voice low. 'She's been with the family all the four years they've been here. Clare was so badly needed in the hospital she went back to work very soon after Jenny was born so Jenny is used to being with Patience most of the time.'

Her blue eyes were shadowed.

'She's so little she'll get over it sooner than the other two,' she said. 'Colin cried a lot at first and that was good, but Sarah—she did cry, but she's too quiet now— almost too good, for a little girl. She's only nine, after all.'

Lesley looked at the brown head, bent industriously over the school-books.

'I think she feels her responsibilities,' she said, and

she thought of Sarah doing what she could to see that Colin and Jenny behaved and said and did what they should.

Sylvia Fraser nodded.

'Yes, I think you're right. But perhaps now that Matt is here she'll be able to see that she can share some of that load with him.' She hesitated. 'And having you here will help, too—help the children, and help Matt.'

She wasn't asking any questions, but somehow Lesley felt she wanted to set the record straight.

'Matt and I have been friends—we've known each other for more than two years now,' she said carefully. 'We were planning to go on a Land Rover trip through Africa when this happened. We had intended coming to Thabanvaba, to work here, and when Matt phoned and said how desperately short-staffed the hospital was I said I'd come. I—don't know how long I'll stay, of course.'

Sylvia smiled.

'My dear, Matt made things very clear when he told us you were coming. I said did this mean we might be having a wedding, and he said no ways. Neither of you were thinking about marriage but you were fond of each other and you were both perfectly happy with the way things were! So, now I've heard it from both of you. I'm very glad you're here.'

She looked at her watch.

'I must go. Ken has a meeting in our house tonight, and I must have supper over before that. Come and visit us, Lesley—we're on the other side of the compound, behind the hospital. Sarah, I'm sure you've done enough homework. I do like your Porsche, Colin. Does the space-captain let anyone else drive it?'

The little boy shook his dark head.

'No, he just likes to drive it himself. It makes a change from his spaceship, you see.'

'I suppose it would,' Sylvia agreed gravely, and for

a moment her eyes met Lesley's, though they both managed to keep their faces straight.

Sarah put her books down, and went inside to bring out her paper dolls. Lesley admired the careful cutting-out, and she and Sarah discussed what other clothes Flora and Fiona might need.

'They have these long evening dresses,' Sarah said, 'but they might need something more—more smart casual.'

'Something like silky trousers—or culottes?' Lesley suggested, and Sarah's face lit up.

'We'll make them next time,' Lesley said. 'Could you organise some plain white paper and paint or crayons? I'm just going to say hi to Jenny before I go.'

'Aren't you going to have supper with us?' Sarah said, but Lesley shook her head.

'Not tonight,' she said.

It was, she was realising, a potentially awkward situation. She had no wish to appear to have a relationship with Matt any different from that of anyone else on the staff of the hospital. The way Anna-Marie Botha had looked at her—the cool hostility in her eyes—had made her see the dangers of that. And yet the other side of the picture was that things *were* different between Matt and her, which was why she was here. But, for a start, she certainly wasn't going to make a habit of eating here with Matt and the children.

'I'm going to the staff dining-room for supper,' she said. And then, seeing the disappointment in Sarah's brown eyes, she went on, 'Some other time, Sarah.'

'We don't always have meatballs and pink pudding, you know,' Colin said. 'Sometimes we have spaghetti, and sometimes we have pizzas from the deep-freeze.'

Lesley assured him that she liked both spaghetti and pizzas, and she would look forward to either.

Jenny was in her high-chair in the kitchen, dipping fingers of French toast into tomato sauce. She offered

Lesley a piece, and she accepted, managing to dispose tactfully of some of the tomato sauce first.

'Tonight she eat first, then bath,' Patience said cheerfully. 'You want more milk, Jenny?'

The little girl nodded, and held out her beaker.

'Now you say, "thank you, Patience",' Patience said, and Jenny said something which seemed to satisfy her.

'You staying here to eat tonight, Miss Lesley?' she said, and Lesley said, no, she was going to the staff dining-room.

She kissed the top of Jenny's fair curly head, and was saying goodbye to Sarah and Colin on the steps of the stoep when Matt hurried in.

'Lesley's not having supper with us tonight, Uncle Matt, but she will another time,' Colin said quickly.

For a moment Matt's eyes met hers questioningly.

'We do need to have a talk about staff and duty times in your ward,' he said.

'I know,' Lesley agreed. 'Perhaps you could come over to the ward tomorrow, Matt?'

It was a moment before he replied.

'Yes, I'll do that,' he said, and then added, smiling, 'That's a good idea, Lesley.'

Lesley was probably right, Matt thought reluctantly.

This was a small hospital, and although everyone knew that Lesley had come because he'd asked her to— because of their—friendship—it was perhaps reasonable that they should keep some sort of professional distance.

Reasonable, but disappointing.

He had been looking forward to seeing Lesley tonight; to telling her about some of the problems he was finding in the hospital; to hearing how she was doing in the maternity ward, even to talking to her about tomorrow's clinic.

And also, he thought, as he and Sarah and Peter sat on the stoep having supper—Jenny, bathed and looking like a small cherub, was already in bed—he had been looking forward to sharing this time with the children with her.

He hadn't known them very well, his two nieces and his nephew, before this. Peter and Clare had been in England on holiday twice in the last few years and he had seen Sarah and Colin then, but he hadn't ever seen Jenny. And now, in this short time, they had become part of his life.

Sometimes—when he looked at Colin playing or lying in bed reading, his small freckled face absorbed— long-forgotten memories of Peter and himself as small boys brought a sudden stab of grief. And Sarah was so like her mother. He hadn't known his sister-in-law very well, but he had liked her, and seeing the love and the closeness between Peter and her had meant a great deal to him. Jenny, little Jenny—there was nothing complicated in his feelings for her. With one dimpled smile, and her chubby arms held out trustingly to him, she had found her place in his heart. A hard-boiled heart, he had always thought it until now.

His day in the hospital had been long and tiring, but he sat down on the floor with Colin to have the space-station explained to him, and he agreed that the space-captain would enjoy driving his Porsche around Venus. Then he sat with Sarah, and listened while she told him what she and Lesley were planning for the paper dolls. And when he had said goodnight to them both he stood in the hall and realised, with wonder and with humility, that he was important to these children— that him being here with them had made a difference to them.

That day at Heathrow last year, when Peter was leaving, they had talked more seriously than ever before, and Peter had said, 'The way things are, Matt, if anything were to happen to Clare and me there would be no one for the children.'

He had explained about Clare's parents.

'Would you take them on, Matt, if they were left on their own?'

Matt, ready to make a light-hearted reply, had seen how serious his brother was.

'Yes, Peter, I would,' he had said.

It was a promise given, and it was a promise he would not—could not—go back on. Even though keeping it had changed his life completely.

There was the giving up of the African dream for Lesley and him. The giving up of his freedom. The unbelievable change in his work—from the huge city hospital in London to this small understaffed mission hospital here in the Transkei.

This was something he very much wanted to share with Lesley. For, in spite of the frustrations of working here, he had to admit that he was enjoying the challenge. Each day held something new, and he had to think fast and act fast. Lesley would find that, too, in the maternity ward and with the clinics, and they could talk about it—share it.

Lesley.

It was only after the children were asleep and he was sitting in the warm darkness of the stoep, alone, that he let himself think of last night when he had kissed her.

It was strange, that.

Until now things between them had been—easy, casual, uncomplicated. No big deal, no deep feelings. But last night—when he had taken Lesley in his arms, when he had kissed her—he wasn't sure just how it was he had felt but, whatever, it had been extremely disturbing.

He found himself wondering if Lesley had found that kiss disturbing, too.

CHAPTER FOUR

IN THREE days, Lesley realised with a shock, it would be the end of November.

And Christmas was just around the corner. The first Christmas without their parents for Sarah and Colin and Jenny. A Christmas Colin thought wouldn't be very nice.

Oh, no, Lesley told herself determinedly. We're not having that. We're going to do our darnedest to see that Christmas is—well, as good a Christmas as we can make it.

Through the day, memories of her own childhood Christmases kept coming to her. The bulging stockings, the Christmas tree with the familiar and loved decorations on it, the three children—herself and her brothers—trying to guess what was in the parcels under the tree. The walk across the snowy field to church. The family meal afterwards.

During the morning Matt came in to the small duty room, where Lesley was checking the drugs cupboard.

'I have my TB clinic in ten minutes,' he said, 'but I thought I'd take the chance to come over now.'

He sat on a corner of the desk.

'I suppose you're going to tell me you need another trained midwife,' he said.

'Yes, I am,' Lesley replied. 'Obviously, having two is better than having only one, and we can manage for a short time, but we must get someone else as soon as possible. Sister Cekiso is going to do nights and I'll do days, but it does mean we've got to be within call any time we're off duty. Sister Cekiso will only be able to go home for a day unless I—yes, I could sleep here in the ward, with a nurse-aide on duty, so that she can have a night at home.'

Matt shook his head.

'All right for a short-term arrangement,' he said, but no more than that. And working all-out like that you're not going to have much time or energy for the children.'

The children.

'Matt,' she said, urgently, 'we've got to think about Christmas.'

'I know,' he replied. 'Look, I know you've got some reservations about professional relationships, but let's get our priorities right, Lesley. The children need more than I can give them, and already they talk so much about you. Please come over tonight—you can have some time with them, and we'll talk about Christmas.'

He was right, Lesley thought, but she remembered the cool hostility on Anna-Marie Botha's face. But, well, the Afrikaans sister was on General so they didn't actually have to work together.

Unconsciously, Lesley lifted her chin.

I can surely take a bit of aggro in my stride, she told herself. I don't think she and I would ever be bosom buddies, anyway.

'I'll come,' she said briefly. 'But, Matt, is there anything we can do about staffing?'

Matt stood up, looking at his watch.

'Ken Fraser is off to Cape Town today,' he told her. 'The mission headquarters are there. He's requesting another doctor and another trained nurse. Anna-Marie needs more staff in General, too. We may have to settle for sharing between Maternity and General. There isn't much money, you see.'

The mission hospital was partly government-funded, he explained, and partly financed by the mission. There was a country-wide shortage of trained medical staff, and a mission hospital in the Transkei, far from anywhere, wasn't the most appealing place.

'We have to have another doctor with experience in

anaesthetics,' he said. 'I desperately need to be able to work under general when it's necessary.'

At the door he turned.

'See you tonight?'

Lesley nodded, and turned back to her checklist for the drugs cupboard.

The clinic was held in a small room beside the maternity ward, and when Lesley went through in the afternoon she left her young nurse-aide, Faith, in charge of the ward. No patient was in labour, and none of the other mothers had any potential problems.

'But I'm right here if you need me,' she told Faith.

There were six—no, seven—women in the small room. One swift glance told Lesley that at least two of them would be delivering very soon. The women, chattering and laughing among themselves, were silent when she went in, but looked at her with great interest.

'I'm Sister Grant,' she said. 'And I'm happy to meet all of you. We'll do the routine check-ups first.'

She was relieved to find that most of her patients understood English. One of the older women needed explanations from her neighbour, but with this help the routine check-ups went smoothly. The charts, she realised with a jolt, must be in Clare's writing. Blood pressure—blood for testing for glycosuria—weight gain—palpitation. Urine tests. She was grateful that these tests could be done right here, although the blood tests had to be sent to a laboratory and any test with a problem had to be sent away.

Two of the young women were here for the first time, and Lesley completed more detailed medical histories for them, although it was a little disconcerting when she wanted an obstetric history to be greeted with a blank look and an admission that the mother didn't remember many details about her two previous births. Lesley did the best she could, and when she had finished the folders she took the time to talk to the women about health in pregnancy. She reminded herself as she started that these women, living in a rural area like this, were considerably less sophisticated than any patients she had ever talked to before.

'You want to have healthy babies,' she said. 'And you want them to grow into healthy children. If you come here regularly we will be able to check that everything is going well with you and with your baby. We can tell if the baby is growing well—we can tell if you need iron.

'If you hear of anyone who has measles, or anyone who has TB, keep away from them.'

One young mother-to-be sat up, her dark eyes anxious.

'Sister, my mother's aunt is ill with the coughing sickness,' she said.

'Then keep away from her until she is well,' Lesley said. 'Does your mother's aunt go to Dr Turner's clinic?'

'Sometimes she go, other times she is too busy. And she is old woman now—she say soon she will die anyway.'

'Tell her—no, tell your mother to tell her—that she must go,' Lesley said sternly. 'Apart from herself, she will make other people ill.' Matt had said TB was a devastating problem—she must talk to him about it.

She told the women about the importance of body-building foods, and about the dangers of smoking and taking drugs of any kind. But she realised, as she told them the right kinds of food to eat, that she was probably being very unrealistic in this poor rural community. And that was something else she must talk to Matt about. And, perhaps, to Sylvia Fraser.

She looked at the charts Clare had left, and saw that there should be four more women here at the clinic. But when she asked the others if they knew why the other women weren't there the only reply she got— and that a vague one—was that it was far to their villages, and perhaps the women didn't have the time to come. Lesley had to give up on that, but it was something else she'd talk to Matt about, she told herself.

After the clinic there was only time to check on her patients, help Faith with the babies' feeding round and check on any drugs to be given before Sister Cekiso arrived to take over.

Lesley took five minutes to hurry to her room and change into a cotton dress, before going across to the house. As she was brushing her hair and putting lipstick on, she thought again of her own memories of Christmas.

And then, her brush poised above her head, another thought came to her.

'These are my memories, my traditions. Sarah and Colin and Jenny must have their own traditions, their own special things.'

Jenny was too sleepy to stay up, Sarah explained when Lesley ran up the steps of the stoep.

'Patience is just putting her to bed, but Patience can't read very well and Mummy or Daddy always read a story to Jenny. I do it sometimes, but—but I thought maybe you could tonight, Lesley?' Sarah asked, and Lesley thought that a little girl of nine shouldn't have to look so anxious.

'I'd like to do that,' she said.

'I'll come and listen, too, though it will be a baby story,' Colin said. 'But I don't mind. I'll just keep you and Jenny company.'

Sarah said she would wait for Uncle Matt, and Lesley and Colin went along to Jenny's room. Jenny was in her cot, but Lesley lifted her out and held her while she read the book Colin had chosen.

'She likes the "Cat in the Hat" books,' he said authoritatively. 'She's too little to understand, acksherly, but she likes the pictures.'

Lesley wasn't so sure about Jenny not understanding because the little girl pointed eagerly to each picture and laughed as the Cat in the Hat tried to get rid of the pink cat spot. But, whether or not Jenny understood, it was very clear that Colin was enjoying the story.

When Lesley closed the book Jenny's dark lashes were almost closed over her blue eyes. It was very pleasant, Lesley thought with some surprise, holding the warm, sleepy baby close to her. She settled Jenny in her cot, with her blanket held close to her, and kissed the fair curly head.

Matt had arrived while she was with Jenny, and he and Sarah were sitting on the swing seat together.

'Jenny asleep? I'll look in on her later,' he said.

He stood up and came over to Lesley and Colin, ruffling Colin's dark hair and then kissing Lesley. A brief, warm kiss, the kind of kiss they always exchanged on meeting, Lesley thought. Not at all like the kiss that had so surprisingly disturbed her.

'No pink pudding tonight, I'm afraid,' he said, and now there was laughter in his dark eyes. 'Colin thought you might like jelly and ice cream instead.'

She had thought that she would talk to Matt after the children were in bed—tell him the thoughts she had had about Christmas—but as Colin finished his ice cream, he said, 'Sarah and Jenny and me have ice cream at Christmas 'cos we don't like brown puddings, like Christmas pudding. Mummy—Mummy and Daddy liked Christmas pudding. Do you like Christmas pudding, Uncle Matt?'

Matt's eyes met Lesley's.

'Yes, I do,' he said, after a moment. 'But I like ice cream, too. We could just have ice cream this Christmas. What do you think, Lesley?'

He was asking for help, she knew that, and not just about Christmas pudding.

'I was thinking about Christmas today,' she said slowly. 'I was remembering the special things my brothers and I used to do. What did you do that was special for Christmas?'

For a moment she thought she had done the wrong

thing as Sarah looked at her, her brown eyes slowly filling with tears.

'Oh, Sarah, love,' she said, not quite steadily, 'I didn't mean to make you sad.'

'Don't cry, Sarah,' Colin said, alarmed.

Lesley put her arms around the child and held her close. But no more tears came, and after a moment Sarah managed to smile.

'I'm not going to cry, Colin,' she said. 'Did you have an advent calendar, Lesley, when you were a little girl?'

'No, we didn't,' Lesley said.

'We always have ours sitting up on the big sideboard,' Sarah told her. 'And we take it in turns to open a little window, not Mummy and Daddy, just Colin and me and Jenny.'

'You start when it's December, and you open one window every day. And last year,' Colin said triumphantly, 'I was the one what opened the Christmas Eve one, the one what has Mary and Joseph and Baby Jesus, and—'

'Don't tell,' Sarah said, and Lesley was glad to see a more normal childish reaction as Sarah frowned at her brother quite fiercely. 'It has to be a surprise.' Her face fell. 'But it doesn't matter because we don't have one, anyway. And it's almost December.'

Too late to get one, Lesley thought. Maybe I can make one.

Above Sarah's brown head Matt's eyes met hers, and she knew he was thinking much the same.

'What else did you do for Christmas?' he asked. 'Did you have a tree?'

'Not a real one—they don't grow here,' Sarah said. 'But we have a pretend one—I think it's in that big trunk in the attic.'

'We'll look in the trunk another day,' Matt promised. 'But anything else you remember—the special things you do for Christmas—tell me or tell Lesley.'

Later, when Sarah and Colin were in bed, he said,

'It's a start, anyway. I like the way you did it, too, Lesley.'

They were sitting on the swing seat, and he put one arm around her lightly, his hand resting on her bare arm.

'I'll try to make some sort of advent calendar,' Lesley said doubtfully.

'Ask Sylvia—she might be able to help us,' Matt suggested, and Lesley thought that was a good idea.

She told Matt about her first clinic, and he confirmed that the blood for testing would be taken to Umtata the next day. He would talk to Ken Fraser about the patients who should have been there, he said, and arrange for someone to go to their villages and talk to them.

'I think you'll find your clinic more rewarding than my TB one,' he said, and he told her that TB was the number one infectious disease killer, not only here in the rural areas of Transkei but in the whole of South Africa.

'Malnutrition, overcrowding in homes and in schools—all that helps to spread it. And then there's the *sangomas*.'

'*Sangomas*?' Lesley asked.

'Herbalists,' Matt said briefly. 'In spite of mission hospitals like ours, in spite of churches, they're still a powerful influence. They treat TB with a course of enemas and emetics, and the patients go around infecting many more people, before they come to us. And even when they do most of them don't stick with their treatment. They get a bit better, then they're discharged from hospital. They're supposed to remain on medication and come back for regular check-ups, but far too many of them don't.'

Peter had written at length about the TB problem, he told her, in his last letter.

'There's a new strategy, but we haven't enough people to use it yet,' he said. 'It's called DOTS, and it means Directly Observed Treatment, Short Course. It needs health workers to watch each patient swallow the correct medication. It's what we need—one of the things we need.' He shrugged. 'Maybe some day. . . Meanwhile, we keep on treating people, trying to make them see that sticking with the treatment is a matter of life or death.'

His arm tightened around her shoulders, drawing her closer.

'Let's talk about something else,' he said. He smiled, but the smile didn't quite reach his dark eyes. 'Most of the time I'm managing to look on the way things are here at Thabanvaba as a challenge. But—sometimes it gets discouraging.'

'What do you want to talk about?' Lesley asked him.

In the dim warm darkness of the stoep he looked down at her.

'Actually,' he said, softly, 'I don't want to talk at all. I had other things in mind.'

He kissed her gently—her eyelids, her cheek and then her mouth. Slowly Lesley felt the tension, of which she had hardly been aware, leaving her, and she returned the warmth of his kiss, loving the dear familiarity of his arms around her—of his lips on hers—in this warm and undemanding way.

And then, suddenly, everything changed. His lips were hard on hers, fierce and demanding, and his arms held her pinned against him. And Lesley found that her heart was thudding unevenly, that she was responding to the urgency of his lips in a way she wouldn't have dreamed possible between Matt and her. And that frightened her.

She drew back and after a moment he released her. But he was still so close that she could hear that his heart, too, was thudding unevenly.

Lesley turned her head away, not wanting to answer the question in Matt's dark eyes.

But he asked her, anyway.

'What's wrong, Lesley?'

She shook her head, and he gave her a little shake.

'Come on,' he said, 'we've always been able to talk, you and I.'

That was true, but that, too, had changed.

'I don't really know,' she said hesitantly. 'I think it's— You've changed, Matt. I feel as if I don't know you any more. You're—different.'

Sometimes you seem like a stranger, she thought. But she didn't say that.

In the warm darkness she heard him sigh.

'I suppose that's true,' he said, after a moment. 'The things that have happened—well, it would be surprising if I hadn't changed. But damn it, Lesley, I don't want things to change between us. We were doing fine just as we were. Weren't we?'

'Yes, we were,' Lesley replied. And then said slowly, as she thought about it, 'But we can't go back. We— we just have to go on from here now.'

She was very conscious of the closeness of his body to hers—of his head turning towards her in the warm darkness.

'If you feel you don't know me any more,' he said, not quite steadily, 'maybe we need to get to know each other all over again.'

He kissed her again, long and deep. And—different, and very, very disturbing, Lesley thought, dazed, when he released her.

'I think I should go,' she murmured, and now the old Matt was there—the Matt she knew—with laughter in his dark eyes and in his voice.

'Maybe you should,' he agreed. 'Because if you don't I might not be answerable for the consequences.'

And neither might I, Lesley thought with honesty.

Matt walked to the gate with her.

'It could be fun, getting to know each other all over again,' he said, and his lips brushed hers lightly, fleetingly, as they parted.

Maybe, Lesley thought later in bed in her room. And, again, maybe not.

The next day she saw Sylvia Fraser crossing the compound, and ran out to catch her.

'An advent calendar?' Sylvia said, when Lesley told her what Sarah had told her. 'I've got some old ones tucked away somewhere, Lesley—we always had them when the children were small. I'll see what I can find.'

The next day she appeared in the staff dining-room when Lesley had just finished having lunch.

'I found one,' she said. 'And just in time since it's the first tomorrow.'

She shook her head.

'I can't remember when we stopped using them—I suppose when the children went to boarding-school. It used to be quite a ritual, each one taking turns to open a little window.'

'We'll be able to start tomorrow,' Lesley said delightedly, looking at the brightly painted advent calendar with its twenty-four little windows. 'It's at least something we can do to make their Christmas as much like Christmas as it can be.'

Sylvia's eyes were shadowed.

'Help them to live with their memories, Lesley,' she said very quietly. 'Memories are—very important, no matter what your age is.'

For a moment Lesley thought she was going to say something else, but she shook her head and then turned away.

Tomorrow night, Lesley thought, we'll open the first window. And—and perhaps Matt is right; perhaps we do need to get to know each other all over again.

There was no time the next morning for Lesley to think either of Matt or of Christmas for when she took over the ward from Sister Cekiso one of the clinic patients who hadn't turned up for her check-up had just come in, already in labour.

'I can stay longer, if you like, Sister Grant,' the sister offered, but Lesley shook her head. 'I was just going to examine her.'

'No, you've had a busy night, with the diabetes patient and the baby who didn't want to feed. How is he now?'

Sister Cekiso smiled.

'He is getting the right idea now, Sister. All right, I'll go, but if you need me send Faith for me.'

It was only afterwards that Lesley realised that Sister Cekiso, like so many experienced nurses—and perhaps midwives most of all—sometimes had a feeling about a patient, a reaction that had nothing to do with science but perhaps everything to do with experience.

'You weren't at the clinic, Mrs Sekala,' she said as she began to examine the young woman.

'No, Sister, my child was sick. I had to stay at home with him,' Mrs Sekala said.

'Is he better now?' Lesley asked. 'Who is looking after him?'

'My mother has come—she lives in the next village and she will stay to help when I go home with the new baby, Sister.'

Lesley went on talking to hide her sudden concern at the baby's position. If that head didn't move—

'Nothing happening at the moment, Mrs Sekala,' she said. 'I think you should have a cup of tea, and I'll check again in a little while.'

Two hours later the baby's head still hadn't moved. Oh, for the miracles of modern science which a big hospital can provide, Lesley thought as she re-checked the foetal heartbeat.

'I'm going to see if Dr Turner can come and have a look at you, Mrs Sekala,' she said. 'It's time this baby was doing something.'

She sent Faith to see if Matt could come, and five

minutes later she heard his voice as he and Faith came in the main door of the ward.

'I'll be back in a moment, Mrs Sekala,' she told her patient, wanting to talk to Matt out of her patient's hearing.

'You need me, Sister?' Matt said, when she reached him.

'Sorry to have to send for you, but I do,' Lesley said. Matt nodded.

'I know you wouldn't unless you had to,' he said. 'What's the problem?'

'Deep transverse arrest,' Lesley said. 'She's well into second stage, and that head just isn't moving. I've been monitoring the foetal heartbeat, and there are now signs of distress.'

'So it looks like a forceps delivery,' Matt said. 'Right, let's go and see her.'

The young woman's dark eyes were anxious as she looked up at the doctor.

'There is something wrong with my baby, Doctor?' she asked.

Matt shook his head. 'Your baby is a little tired, that's all,' he said. 'We're going to have to give you some help, Mrs Sekala.'

'You are going to cut me to bring the baby out?' Mrs Sekala asked anxiously, and Matt shook his head.

'No, we won't have to do that,' he reassured her. For a moment his eyes met Lesley's, and she knew they'd had the same thought—if there should be the need for an emergency Caesarean they were stuck without an anaesthetist.

'You don't have to be put to sleep or anything— we're just going to help this baby out,' she said.

'Everything ready? Good girl,' Matt said, seeing the instruments Lesley had to hand.

'Kielland's forceps?' he asked, and she handed the correct forceps to him. 'I'll have to rotate the baby's head while I deliver.'

They had worked together in St Margaret's on the maternity ward for a short time, but Lesley couldn't remember whether she had seen Matt do a forceps delivery. Now she watched with professional admiration as he eased the baby out of the position that made a normal birth impossible, and then carefully delivered it.

'Well, well, a little girl,' he said, as Lesley lifted the tiny baby, ready to suction her.

In spite of the distressed heartbeat just before the delivery the baby was all right, she saw with relief when she had suctioned her. With a surprisingly loud yell, the baby breathed normally and Lesley handed her, wrapped in a blanket, to the young mother.

'I wanted a little girl, and so did my husband—he will be so pleased,' Mrs Sekala said, and gently, with one finger, she touched her baby's cheek.

When Matt had gone, and Mrs Sekala and her baby— both of them fresh and clean—had been taken through to the ward, Lesley went through to the duty room to fill in her chart for the delivery. To her surprise, Sister Cekiso was there in a brightly flowered dress. She held out a cup of coffee to Lesley.

'You will be needing this, Sister Grant,' she said.

'You're supposed to be sleeping,' Lesley said, as she took the coffee. 'But thanks—I do need it. What are you doing here?'

As she said it she remembered the older woman telling her to send for her if she was needed.

'You knew things weren't right, even without examining her?' she asked, and Sister Cekiso nodded. 'And you came back to check?'

'It's just a feeling—sometimes the feeling is right, sometimes it is wrong. This time it was right,' she said, a little apologetically.

'I know that feeling,' Lesley said slowly. 'I've had it sometimes, too.'

'And you will have it more as you grow older and

have more experience. And each time listen to the feeling,' the African sister told her.

'I certainly will,' Lesley replied. She put down her cup. 'Thanks, Sister Cekiso. Go and have a look at the baby, and then you can go back to sleep.'

'I will do that, but—can we be less formal, you and I? Will you call me Agnes?'

'I'll be pleased to,' Lesley said, and she knew that this meant complete acceptance from this woman who was older, more experienced and from a different culture. 'And my name is Lesley.'

The difficult birth had taken up a good part of the day, and the hours flew by as Lesley and young Faith caught up on the normal ward routine. One of the mothers had diabetes, and had to have her temperature checked four-hourly in case of sepsis. Graduated exercises were required, and she had to be kept ambulant to minimise the risk of thromboembolism, Lesley explained to Faith.

In no time at all, it seemed, Agnes Cekiso was back, ready to take over for the night. Lesley hurried to her room, changed quickly and went off, the advent calendar in a large envelope in her hand.

The three children—and the dog—were waiting for her.

'Jenny slept a long time this afternoon so she can stay up now,' Sarah told her.

'And Uncle Matt's just showering. He's all covered in blood 'cos he had to stitch up a man's leg,' Colin said, with some relish.

'Colin, you shouldn't say things like that,' his sister said. 'It isn't very nice.'

The little boy shrugged. 'So?' he returned. 'Lesley's a nurse. Nurses don't mind blood.'

He was deliberately provoking Sarah, Lesley could see that. Fortunately, Matt came out from the house at that moment and Colin and Jenny ran to him.

'He's an awful boy sometimes,' Sarah said to Lesley,

and she sighed. Like a little old woman, Lesley thought, caught between amusement and compassion.

'It's all right, I don't mind,' she assured Sarah. 'I have two brothers myself, Sarah. I know what boys are.'

Sarah's smile lit up her small face and Lesley, remembering photographs of the girl's mother, could see that Sarah would one day be a lovely woman, and very like her mother. Jenny now, with her fair curls and her blue eyes and her dimples, was very different from either Sarah or Colin.

She said as much to Matt when his kiss brushed her cheek. Jenny, in his arms, held out her own chubby little arms to Lesley.

'You are a poppet,' Lesley said, delighted, kissing the fair curls.' An absolute charmer.'

'Yes, she is different,' Matt said, looking at his small niece. 'She's unbelievably like my mother. Peter saw that right away—that's why she's Jenny, after Mum.'

'So you and Peter were both like your father?' Lesley asked.

'Who's that you're talking about?' Colin demanded.

'Your grandfather—your dad's father, my father,' Matt told him. He looked at the envelope Lesley had put down on one of the stoep chairs. 'This what I think it is?'

Lesley nodded.

'I think now,' Matt said, 'in case Jenny falls asleep in her high chair in spite of the afternoon nap.'

He looked at the children.

'I suppose you know what day it is?' he asked.

'Wednesday,' Colin said, surprised.

'The first of December,' Sarah said quietly, at the same time.

Matt nodded.

'And Lesley has managed to get us an advent calendar.' Lesley took the advent calendar out of the envelope.

'I got it from Sylvia,' she said, as Sarah's brown

eyes gazed at her wonderingly. 'Who's going to open the first little door?'

'We call them windows,' Colin told her.

'Right, windows, then,' Lesley agreed, seeing that even using the right word was important.

'Oldest first?' Matt asked.

Sarah shook her brown head. 'It should be Jenny,' she said. 'The one that starts is the one that gets the special window, and Colin got it last year and I got it the year before. Mummy said—' For a moment there was a break in her voice, then she went on, steady again.

'Mummy said it would be Jenny to start this year.'

'Me do,' Jenny said, catching on.

'That all right with the rest of the team?' Matt asked casually, but his eyes were on Colin.

'It's fair,' the little boy said grudgingly. 'And—and Mummy did say it would be Jenny's turn.'

Jenny's small brown hand was held out eagerly. Lesley sat down on the swing seat with Jenny on her lap.

'Colin, would you show Jenny which one to open?' she suggested. 'Since she's too little to know.'

Colin took his small sister's hand in his, and showed her the window with the number one on it. Jenny, with a little unobtrusive help from Lesley, opened the little cardboard flap.

There was a picture of a black cat sitting beside a glowing fire.

'Pussy,' Jenny said, clearly delighted.

'She said "pussy". Did you hear her—she said it prop'ly?' Colin said. 'Say it again, Jenny, say "pussy".'

'Pussy,' the baby said again, and she pointed to the picture and smiled.

There was a sudden loud bark, and they all looked at the dog as he emerged from under the chintz-covered couch. His ears were alert and his head a little to one side. As they looked at him he growled softly, his tail wagging eagerly.

'It's 'cos we said pussy,' Colin said. 'Where's the pussy, Murray?'

Murray ran to the gate and put his paws on it.

'He likes chasing cats,' Sarah said. 'If he gets out he chases Sylvia's cats. That's why he couldn't come with us when we—when we stayed with Sylvia and Ken. He never catches them, of course, but he gives them a fright.'

'Come back here, Murray, you clown,' Matt said affectionately, and after one last searching inspection of the compound Murray came back, his tail-wagging now a little apologetic.

He went first to Matt, laying his head on Matt's knee and waiting to be patted, then to each of the children in turn. Colin explained that Murray was saying he was sorry to be so silly. Even baby Jenny knew what he expected, Lesley saw. And then he came to her.

'I think he's accepted me,' she said, patting the golden head. 'He's been—sort of pleasant but a little distant until now. What is he, anyway?'

'Part collie, part Alsation, maybe part setter, Peter and Clare thought,' Matt told her.

'And why Murray?' Lesley asked.

'After a dog on TV,' Colin said. 'A dog what gets to lie on beds, and that's what Murray wants to do but we don't let him.'

'Where do we put the advent calendar?' Matt asked, and Sarah and Colin, in unison, told him it had to go on the sideboard in the dining-room. They all went inside, and Matt put the bright calendar in its place.

'Me tomorrow,' Sarah said, ' 'cos we do go oldest to youngest.' And added, with an admonitory glance at Colin, 'Not youngest to oldest.'

Later, when supper was over and the children were in bed, Lesley, saying goodnight to Sarah, said to her quietly, 'I know it hurts, Sarah, doing these special Christmas things without your mummy and your daddy, but—is it better to do them, even if it does hurt?'

Am I going too deep? she wondered, looking at the bent head. She's only nine, after all.

After a moment Sarah looked up.

'Yes, it's better to do them,' she said slowly. 'It—it makes me miss Mummy and Daddy even more, but it would be worse not to do the special Christmas things. You see, Lesley, if we don't do them Jenny won't know about them—she's too little to remember. Colin and me, we'll remember, we'll always remember, but not Jenny.'

Lesley put her arms around the child's shoulders and held her close, her heart aching for Sarah.

'I think that's very wise of you, Sarah,' she said, not quite steadily. 'And I think, too, your mummy and daddy would want you to remember.'

She said goodnight and kissed Sarah, and then she went out to the warm darkness of the stoep. Matt was already there, for both Jenny and Colin had gone to sleep very quickly, and she told him what Sarah had said.

He shook his head.

'It's tough for them,' he said. He moved along, and she sat down beside him on the swing seat. 'I'm so glad you're here for Sarah, Lesley. I'm a bit at a loss with her sometimes—she's such a serious little thing. I can understand Colin better, of course.'

'Colin is very like you,' Lesley said, and she remembered the way the little boy had shrugged, the way his eyebrows drew together. Even his smile was like Matt's.

'We're—we were very like each other, Peter and I,' Matt said. He smiled. 'He gets a bit bolshy sometimes, and I can relate to that, too.'

'Oh, yes,' Lesley agreed, looking at him under her lashes, 'you can be very bolshy sometimes, Dr Turner.'

It was very pleasant, she thought drowsily a little later, sitting here in the warm darkness with Matt's arms around her and his lips on hers in a warm, satisfying kiss, but a kiss that wasn't either disturbing or threatening. This is how it should be for Matt and me, she thought. This is how it was before.

'I should be going,' she murmured at last, regretfully.

'I suppose you should,' Matt agreed, but he made no move to release her.

'Really,' Lesley said more forcefully, and she managed to free herself. Matt walked to the gate with her.

'I'm so glad you thought of finding out their special Christmas things,' he said. 'We'll find a tree, and nearer Christmas we can decorate it. Sylvia was telling me there's a Christmas party for all the children from the mission station and from the villages on Christmas Eve. Apparently, Ken does a good line in being Father Christmas.'

Lesley looked up at him.

'Sylvia and Ken are obviously fond of the children,' she said, 'and they took them right away after the accident. I know it's a lot for people who aren't family to take on, but I wonder if they thought of taking them for good?'

It was a little while before Matt said anything.

'I don't think Sylvia would mind me telling you,' he said slowly. 'I think she'd probably tell you herself at the right time. She has cancer, Lesley. She had a mastectomy a year ago. She's had chemotherapy but there are secondaries. She's on treatment and she has regular check-ups in Umtata but the prognosis isn't too good.'

She talked about memories being important, Lesley thought, remembering. She was thinking about herself—about her own children.

'Will you tell her that you've told me?' she said, not quite steadily, and Matt said that he would.

A day or two later, when Ken Fraser came back from Cape Town, Lesley and Matt were invited to have supper with them. Lesley, arriving at their house as soon as she could after coming off duty, found that Matt was already there.

'A quick clinic for once,' he said. He shook his head. 'More of a casualty department today, actually. I should have had about twenty people here for TB check-ups. Instead I had eight, plus one man who had gashed his leg on a scythe, a woman with a broken wrist and three children with burns. We get too many burns, Ken.'

'I know we do, Matt,' Ken Fraser replied. 'I don't like to say it, but wait until winter when all these huts have paraffin stoves. Then you'll know all about burns. Anyway, I have news that will cheer you up. Cheer both of you up,' he said, and he smiled at Lesley.

'In a week you have an assistant coming, Matt. Young fellow—even younger than you—but he's been doing anaesthetics at Groote Schuur. David Balfour, his name is. His mother is a cousin of the chairman of our board, and apparently David has always been interested in the work we do here. And that's not all. Coming on the same plane is a fully qualified midwife. You'll have to share her with General,' he said quickly. 'I wasn't able to get them to agree to funding two. So you and Anna-Marie can sort that out.'

Lesley couldn't help having a momentary qualm at that, but not enough to take the edge off this good news. And she was even more pleased for Matt.

'You'll be able to do so much more with an anaesthetist here,' she said. 'And if we do need an emergency Caesar—'

'I can't say I'll be jumping for joy at the thought of doing an emergency Caesar,' Matt said, 'but it really will be marvellous to be able to handle more here. That fellow the other day, who had to be taken to Umtata for an appendectomy—I was worried about that three-hour journey, and I knew I could have had his appendix whipped out in no time here.'

'Before you start going into details, let's eat,' Sylvia said, holding up one hand.

She brought out a chicken casserole, a pot of rice and a big bowl of salad.

'Apple pie,' Matt said with delight later. There was laughter in his dark eyes. 'Lesley, can you bear to miss out on pink pudding?'

'You have to eat it more often than I do,' Lesley pointed out.

When they had finished she carried the empty plates through to the kitchen, where Sylvia was making coffee.

'Thanks, Lesley,' Sylvia said. 'Can you take that tray with the cups through, please?'

But as Lesley lifted the tray, the older woman said, very quietly, 'I'm glad you know, Lesley. It makes things easier for me. I was waiting for the right time to tell you, but I'm glad Matt did it for me.'

'I'm so sorry, Sylvia,' Lesley said, knowing how inadequate the words were.

Sylvia lifted her chin.

'I'm not giving up,' she said. 'No ways. There's a new cocktail of drugs I've read about—the doctor in Umtata is trying to get hold of it for me.' She smiled, but the smile didn't quite reach her eyes, Lesley thought. 'Let's take the coffee through. I'm sure you and Matt don't want to be too late.'

'She's very brave and positive,' Lesley said to Matt later, as they walked across the compound together.

'Yes, she is,' Matt agreed. He looked down at her. 'But she does have her bad moments, and I think she'll be glad to talk to you then.'

They had reached the hospital steps, and they both stopped.

'That was a good idea you had,' he said, 'coming over at lunchtime for the opening of the little window. Colin would have hated it if you'd missed it when it was his turn!'

He kissed her. His lips were warm on hers, his arms holding her close to him for a moment then releasing her.

'Goodnight, Lesley,' he said.

Lesley watched his tall figure crossing the compound in the moonlight. That's what I wanted, she told herself. Back on our old casual footing.

So why, she wondered, did she find herself thinking of how she had felt when he had kissed her in a way that was so different, so disturbing?

CHAPTER FIVE

THIS is not easy, Matt thought when he left Lesley, and that's the understatement of the year.

It's darned difficult going back to the way we were before. Kissing her as if she was my best pal—well, perhaps not quite that—holding her lightly, casually.

And letting her go—when everything in me longs to hold her, to feel her body respond to mine the way she did before she drew back.

Take a deep breath or a cold shower or maybe both, he told himself.

He wasn't sure when or how this had happened, this unbelievable change in the way he felt about Lesley. Sure, he'd missed her when he came here to Thabanvaba and he'd been mighty glad to see her, but he hadn't expected to feel quite that glad.

And it wasn't only the physical thing that had changed. There were other disturbing things, too. The way he felt when he saw her sitting with little Jenny on her lap, her cheek against the baby's fair curly head. The other night, when Lesley and Sarah were making clothes for the paper dolls and talking so seriously about the design and the colour. And Colin, turning after his casual 'goodnight' to give Lesley a quick hug.

In all the months—almost two years, he realised—that he and Lesley had known each other their relationship had been so easy, so undemanding. They had established the ground rules right at the start, and they had both been happy about that. Even when they'd been planning their over-Africa trip neither of them had seen that as anything more significant than something they would enjoy doing together.

Peter had asked him, on the phone a few months ago, whether he saw this as a make or break thing.

'Not at all,' Matt had replied instantly, surprised. But it must be difficult for Peter, he had thought—the way he and Clare had felt about each other right from the start—to understand. 'Look, Peter, we don't really see things as going any further than they are right now, Lesley and I. We enjoy each other's company—we're fond of each other—we get on well in every way.'

Over the miles, Peter had said something.

'I didn't catch that,' Matt had said truthfully, 'but I can guess at it. Yes, I do mean every way. But, heck, Peter, that doesn't mean we want to spend the rest of our lives together.'

And now? he thought. Do I want to spend the rest of my life with Lesley? He wasn't too sure about that, but it was a thought which was far from unpleasant. A thought that remained with him when he fell asleep.

The next day was Saturday, and with no school for the children he had been trying to make a later start going over to the hospital at the weekends so that he could at least spend a little more time with them.

Before he opened his eyes he was all too conscious that he was being watched. And, sure enough, when he gave in and opened his eyes two pairs of eyes were fixed unwaveringly on him. Colin's, and the dog's.

Instantly the dog wagged his tail and Colin's small freckled face broke into a wide smile.

'He's awake—Uncle Matt's awake,' he shouted, and Matt tried not to wince.

The next moment Sarah and Jenny came in, both in shortie pyjamas and bare feet, Jenny's small bottom well padded with her night nappy.

'I was just going to dress Jenny,' Sarah said.

'Up,' Jenny said imperiously, holding out her chubby little brown arms. 'Up, Uncle Matt.'

Matt lifted her up beside him, and patted the bed.

'You might as well all join me,' he said. 'No, not you, Murray. Down!'

Obedient, but not at all crushed, the dog lay down on the rug beside the bed with his golden eyes fixed on Matt. As if he'll force me to change my mind about letting him up, Matt thought.

'Could we talk about Christmas presents?' Sarah asked a little shyly.

'Christmas presents,' Matt repeated, taken aback. I wish Lesley was here, he thought fervently, and then he looked at the bed, himself and three children—with the dog beside them—and smiled. But I still wish she were here, he thought!

'Christmas presents,' he said again, trying to sound bright and cheerful because this was something that hadn't crossed his mind.

'We sometimes used to go to Cape Town or Durban to get presents for each other, and to Look At Things,' Colin said, and Matt could hear the importance of the last three words.

'You mean to look at things you might want for Christmas?' he asked, and Colin nodded.

'But it was mostly so that we could get things to give each other and to give—to give Mummy and Daddy,' Sarah explained. Colin's scathing look told Matt that the little boy's interest had been considerably more in what he wanted to choose for himself, and he had to hide a smile.

There was something very pleasant about the three small bodies close to him, the three small faces turned trustingly up to his. I like these kids, Matt thought. And then—no, I love these kids.

He sat up in bed, and looked from Sarah to Colin and then to Jenny.

'Look,' he said, carefully, 'the way things are at the hospital there's no way we can manage a trip to either Cape Town or to Durban. We just might manage to go to Umtata in the next couple of weeks after the new doctor gets here. I'm not promising, but we'll see what we can do.'

Colin wasn't giving up on this.

'And when we know what we want,' he said, 'we write letters. To Father Christmas.'

'You write letters to Father Christmas,' Matt said. 'And then you post them?'

The little boy shook his dark head.

'No one acksherly posts letters to Father Christmas,' he explained patiently. 'It doesn't work like that. We write our letters, and—' He turned to Sarah. 'Will you help me again with the difficult words, Sarah?'

Sarah nodded.

'We put our letters on the coffee-table,' Colin went on, 'and we put out a glass of milk and some biscuits, and do you know what, Uncle Matt?'

He paused and took a deep breath.

'The next morning the letters are gone and the milk is finished, and some of the biscuits,' he said impressively. 'Father Christmas takes the letters away, and sometimes you get what you ask for but sometimes you don't. You just have to wait and see. Last year Sarah wanted a horse, but she didn't get it.'

'But I did get some of the other things I wanted,' Sarah said quickly.

There was a knock at the door, and when Matt replied Patience opened it.

'You want tea in bed, Dr Matt?' she said. 'Or you want breakfast soon?'

'Breakfast soon, thanks, Patience,' Matt said. 'Right, you lot. Off and get dressed, I want you all ready for breakfast by the time I'm showered and shaved.'

I'll talk to Lesley later, he decided under the shower, and we'll work out something about this Christmas present business.

As for anything else to do with Lesley—there was nothing he could do about it right now, he told himself.

*　　*　　*

There was a sudden and easy birth just when Lesley was about to go off duty and she reached the house too late to bath the children, as she had planned to.

'Patience is seeing to them—I want to talk to you, anyway, before they come through,' Matt said.

'Yes, we used to write letters, too,' Lesley said, when he told her what the children had said. 'I should have thought of that. What about this trip to Umtata, Matt? Can we manage that?'

'We might,' Matt said, 'after this young fellow arrives—and the new nurse. As long as there was nothing desperate happening here—and, of course, there's no guarantee that that wouldn't happen out of the blue—either on the general side or on Maternity. If we made an early start we could get there and back in a day. But there's something else I want to do, too, Lesley, when he gets here. There are a couple of villages over the hills and into the next valley. I'd like to get there, do some TB checks, and I'd like you there, too, to talk to the women—find out if there's anyone who should be coming to the clinics.'

They were on the stoep, waiting for the children to finish bathing and open the next window of the advent calendar.

'Sounds a good idea,' Lesley said. 'That way I could talk to them about birth control. We could take Depo-Provera with us, Matt. Anyone who agrees could have the three-month injection. It would be a great chance to reach women we might not otherwise see.'

'Don't get too carried away,' Matt advised. 'Remember, Lesley, the more rural the area the more likely they are to feel they should have plenty of children. Anyway, we'll aim for getting there. It would mean we'd have to stay overnight, of course.'

Lesley wondered about the children if they did that, but Matt said Patience would be there and Sylvia would keep an eye on them for the two days.

Three clean and shining children came out, with

Patience running after them, brush in hand, to tidy Colin's dark hair, newly washed and standing on end.

'Stand still, Colin, while I make you look nice,' she said sternly.

'I don't want to look nice,' Colin returned.

'I've never seen your Uncle Matt come out of the shower without tidying his hair,' Lesley commented.

Colin looked at Matt.

'Your hair isn't very tidy now,' he said, and Lesley had to smile because Matt had just run a hand through his thick dark hair and it actually looked much like his small nephew's did.

'Let me see what I can do,' she said, and Patience willingly handed her the brush. Colin stood still, his eyebrows drawn together in a way that made him look very like Matt. Matt being bolshy about something, Lesley thought, and she thought that probably Matt, as a little boy, must have looked exactly like Colin did now.

'There, that's better,' she said, and she inspected Colin. 'I wouldn't say you look nice, Colin, I'd say you look cool.'

Colin nodded grudgingly, and had an unobtrusive look at himself in the mirror just inside the door.

Jenny took Lesley's hand, still holding the brush. 'Uncle Matt nice, too,' she said, and she smiled when Lesley tidied Matt's hair.

It was Jenny's turn again to open the little window in the advent calendar, and Sarah and Colin were close to her to see what the picture behind it was.

'A snowman,' Colin said. 'And birds on his head.'

'They're robins,' Sarah told him. 'You get them in places where you get snow.' She looked at Lesley. 'Have you seen snow, Lesley?'

'Have I seen snow?' Lesley said feelingly, remembering the previous winter and the way it had seemed to go on and on. 'And I've made snowmen, too, just like this one.'

Matt was holding the calendar.

'Your daddy and I used to make snowmen,' he said slowly. 'Even when we were almost grown-up we still liked making snowmen. We used to keep an old hat and a scarf and a pipe in the garden shed, and when the first real snow of the winter came we made our snowman. I bet your daddy had photos of some of our snowmen—we'll look in that box of old photos later.'

For a moment his lean dark face was still, his dark eyes shadowed.

I think of the children losing their parents and the sadness they feel, Lesley thought, remorseful, but too often I forget what it's like for Matt, losing his brother.

She put her hand over his. He looked up, and after a moment smiled and the shadows left his eyes.

'Thanks, Lesley,' he said softly.

But it wasn't only Matt who had been affected by memories. When Lesley went to say goodnight to Colin he had switched off his bedside light and his face was turned into the pillow.

'I'm sleeping,' he said, but there was something about the muffled voice, about the small huddled figure, that made Lesley sit down on the bed beside him. When she touched him the small shoulders were rigid.

'I said I'm sleeping,' the little boy said.

Lesley hesitated. Then a small stifled sound from Colin made her forget any uncertainty. She put her arms around him. For a moment he resisted, and then he began to cry. She held him close to her until the heartbroken sobs eased, and then she smoothed the dark hair back from his hot little forehead.

'It was 'cos we were talking about Daddy, and then I was thinking, and—and I don't like thinking about Christmas things and Mummy and Daddy not being here,' Colin managed to say, gulping a little.

'I know,' Lesley murmured, and she held him again. 'There isn't anything we can do to change that, Colin, but I do think your mummy and daddy would want you to have as good a Christmas as we can make it. And it's all right to cry—sometimes it helps.'

The dark eyes, so like Matt's, studied her face.

'Big boys don't cry,' Colin said uncertainly.

You're only a little boy, Lesley wanted to say, her heart aching for him. But she knew that was the wrong thing to say so she told him that sometimes it was all right even for big boys to cry.

'I feel better now,' he said after a while, 'but can Murray stay with me?'

'He can stay, but on the floor,' Lesley said firmly. Murray wagged his tail and Colin nodded, and she thought, So what if Murray does end up on the bed with Colin if that helps?

Telling Matt about this took some time, and it was later than Lesley had intended when she went back to her room in the nurses' home. All the other rooms but Anna-Marie's were in darkness. Lesley went into the tiny kitchen to make herself a cup of tea after she had bathed, and just as the kettle boiled Anna-Marie came in.

'Water boiling, if you want some tea,' Lesley said brightly, determined to ignore the coolness on the girl's face.

'You must have come in very quietly,' the dark-haired girl remarked, taking a teabag from the box in the cupboard. 'Last night or the night before I heard you and Dr Turner laughing quite loudly just outside my window.'

To her annoyance, Lesley could feel her face grow warm.

'I'm sorry if we disturbed you,' she said, hoping she didn't sound as defensive as she felt.

Anna-Marie shrugged,

'*Maak nie saak nie,*' she said. 'Oh, you don't speak Afrikaans. It doesn't matter.'

I might as well take the chance now, Lesley thought.

'Good news that we're getting another nurse, isn't it?' she said.

'Yes, it is. You probably heard before I did, of course. I believe you and Dr Turner were visiting the Frasers the night Ken got back,' the Afrikaans nurse said coolly.

Lesley lifted her chin.

'Yes, I probably did,' she agreed, and she hoped she sounded just as cool. 'I believe we'll have to share her between General and Maternity, but we can work that out.'

The other girl, her back turned, said something that Lesley didn't catch. For a moment she wondered if she should just leave it because she had a feeling she might not like what Anna-Marie had said. But ignoring something that might be unpleasant didn't seem right.

'I'm sorry, I didn't hear what you said,' she said, as pleasantly as she could.

Anna-Marie turned round. 'I said I'd be lucky to see much of her in General.'

'What makes you think that?' Lesley asked.

The Afrikaans girl shrugged. 'I haven't as much influence as you do,' she said.

Lesley felt her cheeks grow warm. She took a deep breath.

'Look, Anna-Marie,' she said, and she hoped her voice was steady, 'as you know very well, Matt and I have been friends for years. Good friends,' she added, knowing she sounded more than a little defiant. 'But our friendship makes no difference at all to our professional relationship. And it will certainly not mean that I get more than my fair share of our extra nurse. I'm sure that Matt intends having a meeting—the three of us— to discuss the best arrangement we can make.'

And I'll certainly see, she thought, that Matt does that, whether he intended to or not.

Impulsively she held out her hand.

'I can see it must have been difficult for you,' she said, 'seeing that the new doctor and the new sister were friends. But surely that needn't make any difference to—to a working relationship between you and me?'

There was no change in the coolness in the other girl's dark eyes and there was no answering smile, although she did take Lesley's outstretched hand.

'We'll see,' she said uncompromisingly, and she took her mug of tea and went out. A moment later Lesley heard the door of her room close.

Oh, well, she told herself philosophically, I've done what I can. Maybe things will be better when the new doctor and nurse arrive.

A few days later she had just finished lunch when one of the nurse-aides looked in to say that the Land Rover had arrived from Umtata. Ken Fraser had gone off that morning to meet the Cape Town plane bringing the doctor and the nurse.

'Dr Matt has gone out to meet them. He's talking to them now,' Jane Sipilo reported from the window. 'Aren't you going out, too, Sister Grant?'

If Anna-Marie hadn't been in the dining-room as well Lesley thought she might have gone. But with the dark girl sitting at the other end of the table, steadfastly drinking her coffee, she shook her head and said that probably Dr Turner would bring the new doctor and nurse in to have something to eat, and they'd all meet them then.

A few moments later the door opened, and Matt and Ken Fraser came in.

'Any food for hungry travellers?' Matt asked. 'There is? Good. Ken, you don't need to hang on—we can look after them.'

Ken Fraser, with a nod to Lesley and Anna-Marie, turned and hurried out, and a tall, fair-haired young man came in.

'David, meet the girls who really call the shots around here,' Matt said. 'Sister Botha and Sister Grant—

Anna-Marie and Lesley. This is Dr Balfour—David.
We don't have time for much in the way of formality
here, David.'

'That suits me,' the young doctor said.

He shook Anna-Marie's hand. 'Nice to meet you,
Anna-Marie.'

Then he turned to Lesley, his deep blue eyes openly
admiring.

'Well,' he said, smiling, 'here I was thinking I was
making all sorts of sacrifices by coming to Thabanvaba,
but somehow I think it's going to be even more interesting than I had expected.'

With some difficulty Lesley extricated her hand.

'We all find our work here interesting,' she said,
more amused than anything else. 'I have to get back to
my ward.'

As she turned away she was all at once very conscious
of Anna-Marie's dark eyes resting on her with more
than the usual coolness.

But not only Anna-Marie's eyes.

She had a moment of shock for she had never seen
Matt look quite like that—dark, unsmiling.

Like a stranger, she thought, more shaken than she
would have thought possible.

I must have imagined it, Lesley thought, bewildered,
as Matt turned smilingly to say something to the young
doctor. We're not like that, Matt and I. We don't keep
tabs on each other. We don't regard each other as private
property in any way. We've always been free, uncom-
mitted.

No, she was certain she must have been wrong about
the way Matt looked when David Balfour had been so
openly admiring. Because there was no doubt that Matt
was very glad to have David there.

'He's a very competent anaesthetist,' Matt said a
few days later, when he and David had dealt in quick
succession with an appendectomy, a broken ankle and

two burn cases which would have been unbelievably traumatic without a general anaesthetic.

'You sound surprised,' Lesley said. 'He's only a few years younger than you are, and I gather his training and his experience at Groote Schuur couldn't be bettered anywhere.'

Matt smiled.

'You gather that from Anna-Marie, I suppose,' he replied, and Lesley nodded. 'How is it working out with Peggy Thorpe splitting her week between General and Maternity?'

'All right,' Lesley said, and it was working out— most of all, she thought, due to Nurse Thorpe's cheerful good nature and her ability to treat everyone pleasantly. But she couldn't help thinking that Peggy Thorpe, who was over forty and a little stout, wasn't the sort of nurse Anna-Marie would take exception to in any way.

The day after that Lesley herself had a chance to see David Balfour's professional ability.

When she took over from Agnes Cekiso in the morning the older sister was concerned about a patient who had come in just after midnight.

'She is still in second stage, Lesley,' she said. 'I have set up an oxytocin drip and IV fluid, but I am not happy about her.'

There was no foetal distress at that stage, but an hour later Lesley checked the dilatation of the cervix, the young mother's blood-pressure and then the foetal heartbeat. She glanced at the chart and then re-checked.

And she remembered, as she did so, her old obstetrics lecturer saying, 'Whatever you do in the labour ward, don't do or say anything that might worry your patient. Sure, if there's something wrong she has to know, but you have to keep her as calm as possible.'

The foetal heartbeat was below a hundred and twenty beats a minute now. She turned to the young nurse.

'We're going to stop the oxytocin drip, Nurse,' she said. 'We'll leave the IV fluid. Mrs Sipanwe, your baby is getting a little tired. I'd like Dr Turner to come and have a look at you. Nurse, could you ask him to come over, please?'

She knew by the widening of young Faith's dark eyes that the girl appreciated the urgency she had managed to keep from her voice. A few minutes later she was back, with Matt striding in behind her.

'Sister—Mrs Sipanwe—let's see how this baby's doing. Foetal heartbeat, Sister?'

Lesley had just re-checked.

'Almost a hundred now, Doctor,' she told him. 'Dropped from a hundred and twenty five minutes ago.'

Matt's eyes met hers for a moment, and then he began to examine the young woman, talking easily to her.

'Mrs Sipanwe,' he said, 'your baby is getting tired so we're going to have to help.' And as the young woman's eyes widened he put his hand over hers. 'Yes, we're going to cut the baby out—we have to. Now, I'm going to give you an injection to make you sleepy.'

He turned to Faith.

'Dr Balfour is in Casualty,' he said. 'Please tell him I need him over here right away.'

By the time David Balfour arrived in the small labour room Lesley had prepared her patient and checked the theatre tray, realising with a shock that probably the last time a Caesar had been done was when Peter and Clare had been here.

She knew how incredibly quick a Caesarean section had to be, and as soon as Mrs Sipanwe was unconscious David put the mask on her.

'She's all yours,' he said to Matt, his voice low. 'She's stable.'

His eyes were on his patient all the time as he maintained her at the fairly light level necessary. Matt, working swiftly, made the first incision, exposed the uterus and lifted the baby out—a boy. Lesley took him, and as she suctioned and aspirated him she was conscious of Matt's hands moving efficiently, doing the

first deep stitches to close the wound and then the neat
stitching of the final layer.

'How's the baby?' he asked then.

'He's fine,' Lesley told him. 'Colour good, breathing
normal.'

'We got him out just in time,' Matt said. 'Thanks,
David—that was a good job.'

He turned to Lesley.

'You know what to do, Sister,' he said. 'Keep her
on her side with a pillow under her shoulders. Set up
an IV drip of glucose. Pulse every fifteen minutes for
three hours, and you'll be watching for any sign of
haemorrhage.'

'And blood pressure now, and then every two hours?'
Lesley asked, and he nodded, his theatre gown already
off and his gloves discarded. And his thoughts, she was
certain, already back in Casualty.

'I'll be back later to check on the baby,' he said.
'Come on, David—we have quite a few folk waiting
for us.'

At the door David Balfour turned.

'She should be coming round soon, Sister,' he said.
'Let me know if there are any post-anaesthetic
problems.'

'I'm glad you were here so that Matt could do the
Caesar,' Lesley said, knowing all too well how bleak
the picture would have been for the baby, and perhaps
for the young mother too, if the anaesthetist hadn't
been here.

'I'm glad, too,' the young doctor said, and he smiled,
adding jauntily, 'See you, Sister.'

Now that Peggy Thorpe was here, Lesley managed
most evenings to leave her ward on time and to go over
to have supper with Matt and the children. Sometimes
little Jenny was already in bed, but Sarah and Colin
were always waiting for her. And the dog.

'I'm sorry I didn't manage to come over at lunchtime
today,' Lesley said on the day of the Caesar, for she

hadn't wanted to leave her patient. 'What was in the little window?'

'We saved it for tonight,' Sarah told her. 'Jenny's almost ready for bed, but Uncle Matt said we'd wait and do it right away before we have supper.'

Patience came out at that moment with a small pyjama-clad figure in her arms.

'Lesley,' Jenny said clearly, and she held out her arms. Lesley took her, loving the warm sweetness of the child in her arms.

'That was quite a day, wasn't it?' Matt said, coming out. 'Hello, sweetheart.'

He dropped a kiss on the baby's head.

'I thought you meant Lesley,' Sarah said, and she giggled, her cheeks pink.

Good, Lesley thought, delighted to see something beyond the quiet and anxious little girl Sarah so often seemed to be.

'Oh, I meant Lesley, too,' Matt assured her. 'See?' And he kissed Lesley's cheek.

'Yes, it was quite a day,' Lesley agreed. 'Thank goodness David was here to do the anaesthetic.'

'We would have been in trouble without him,' Matt said. 'He's very competent.' And then, casually, commented, 'Seems to fit in well with everyone, too. Do you find that?'

'I don't see much of him,' Lesley said, 'other than occasionally in the dining-room, but, yes, everyone seems to like him.'

For a moment, unbidden, came the memory of that strange moment when the young doctor arrived and Lesley had seen Matt as if he was a stranger, his eyes dark and unsmiling.

No, she told herself again as he told Sarah about the operation and David Balfour's skill as an anaesthetist, I must have imagined it. It must have been the way the light was, or something.

'And is the baby all right?' Sarah asked.

'The baby's fine,' Lesley said. 'You can come over and see him tomorrow, if you like.'

'The advent calendar,' Colin put in, obviously impatient with this talk about babies. 'It's my turn.'

He opened the little window, Sarah and Jenny peering over his shoulder.

'Look,' he said, showing the picture to Lesley. It was a family decorating a Christmas tree—the mother kneeling on the floor and the father on a stool, with two children beside him.

'What's the mummy doing?' Colin asked.

'She's taking the decorations out of a box,' Sarah told him.

Little Jenny looked again at the calendar, and pointed with her small brown hand.

'Mummy,' she said.

And then, with bewilderment in her blue eyes, she said it again.

'Mummy? Where Mummy? Where Daddy?'

She looked around.

Lesley knelt down beside her and put her arms around the child.

'Mummy and Daddy aren't here, Jenny,' she said, as steadily as she could. 'But Uncle Matt's here, and I'm here, and—and Sarah's here, and Colin.'

'And Murray,' Sarah said quickly. The dog wagged his tail at the sound of his name.

'Sit, Murray,' Sarah said to the dog. 'Now shake hands with Jenny. That's a good dog.'

The golden dog offered the little girl a paw, and after a moment she laughed and took his paw in her hand.

'I think she'll be all right now,' Sarah said to Lesley, as Jenny went off, her hand in Matt's, to get a biscuit to reward Murray. 'Sometimes she thinks about Mummy and Daddy, but she forgets quite soon.'

And once again Lesley's heart ached for the responsible, grown-up tone of Sarah's voice.

'We've got the tree and the ornaments,' Colin told her then, 'but we're not going to put it up yet.'

'You only do that a week before Christmas,' Sarah reminded him. 'Just about the same time we write our letters.'

'Yes, we have to think about that shopping trip,' Lesley said.

Colin ran to the door, and then came back.

'Uncle Matt's still in the kitchen so we can tell Lesley,' he said. 'Lesley, do you know what we're giving him for Christmas?'

Lesley shook her head.

'I can't begin to guess,' she said truthfully.

'Wooden things what hold books,' Colin told her.

'Bookends,' Sarah explained. 'Ken is helping Colin to make them, and I'm going to paint designs on them when they're finished.'

She hesitated.

'We were doing them for Daddy,' she said, not quite steadily. 'Before—before the accident Colin started them. And then he didn't want to make them, but Ken said—

'I wanted to frow them away,' Colin said vehemently, and the small lapse from the way he usually talked went right to Lesley's heart. 'But Ken said it would be a good idea to do them for Uncle Matt.'

'I think it's a lovely idea,' Lesley assured them. 'And I just know Uncle Matt will love them.'

The children were sitting one on each side of her on the swing seat, and she put her arms around them and hugged them.

Matt, coming out to the stoep, stopped.

Lesley's arms were around Sarah and Colin, holding them close to her, and her eyes were suspiciously bright.

'What will Uncle Matt love?' he asked.

'Nothing,' Sarah said quickly.

'You weren't s'posed to hear,' Colin told him.

Lesley smiled.

'Secrets,' she said. 'Everyone has secrets at this time of year—you should know that. Haven't you got any secrets, Matt?'

'Maybe I do,' Matt replied.

And he thought, Perhaps the biggest secret is the way I feel about you, Lesley.

He was ashamed of that sudden and unexpected reaction he'd had when David Balfour had made it all too clear that he found Lesley attractive. And tonight, when he had tried to sound her out about the young doctor. . .

What's got into me? he wondered. Surely I can take something like that in my stride without feeling this way?

Because this wasn't the way things were between Lesley and him. He remembered last year's hospital ball when he had been called to the theatre. When he'd come back Lesley had been dancing with Craig Hilton from Orthopaedics, the recognised hospital Casanova. Dancing very close together.

And I didn't feel a thing, he remembered now. It didn't bother me one bit.

'Matt, you're miles away,' Lesley said, moving herself and the children to make room for him on the swing seat beside them.

'Thinking about that village trip we're going to make,' he told her with complete untruth.

'Do it soon, Uncle Matt,' Colin urged. 'And then we can go to Umtata. Because it isn't long till Christmas, you know.'

'I'm not forgetting that.' Matt assured him. 'I can't, of course, because every little window we open tells me that it's coming closer.'

'That's what it's meant to do,' Colin told him. 'But you can't cheat, you know.'

'One year Colin opened all the little windows because he thought it would make Christmas come sooner,' Sarah explained.

Above the little boy's dark head Lesley's eyes met

his, and he could see that there was a smile hiding behind her suddenly-tight lips.

'You're growing your hair,' he said, seeing that her fair curls were almost at her shoulders.

'I need to have it cut,' she replied, pushing her hair back. 'But I haven't found the local hairdresser yet.'

'It's Sylvia,' Sarah told her. 'She cuts everyone's hair. She'll do yours, too, Uncle Matt. Can I come with you and watch, Lesley, when Sylvia cuts your hair?'

'Of course,' Lesley replied. 'I must get it done right away. I think short hair is the best in heat like this.'

Matt reached across Colin, and touched a curl of fair hair.

'I like it like that,' he said.

Lesley's grey eyes were startled, and he saw slow warm colour creep into her cheeks.

'You're blushing,' he said, delighted. 'I've never seen you blush before.'

'You've never been in the habit of saying things to make me blush,' Lesley countered.

I don't suppose I have, Matt thought. But, then, I've never felt this way about you before.

This way?

His own thought came back to him, as if he had spoken the words aloud.

'Patience has put Jenny to bed,' he said briskly. 'She was almost asleep on her feet. As soon as we've eaten you two must get off, too—still school for a few days.'

Colin was also fighting sleep by the time supper was over, and soon he was in bed.

'You know what, Uncle Matt?' he said drowsily, when Matt was saying goodnight to him. The dark, heavy-lidded eyes looked up into Matt's.

'We were talking about Christmas, Lesley and Sarah and me, and I was thinking it won't be nice without Mummy and Daddy—I know that, but. . .but it will still be Christmas, won't it?'

Matt kissed his small nephew's freckled nose.

'Yes, Colin, it will still be Christmas,' he said, and he knew his voice was less than steady.

'And we've got to achieve that,' he said to Lesley later, when he told her. In the now-dim light of the warm darkness he looked at her.

'I'm asking a lot of you,' he said. 'Workwise, yes, I knew that, but with the children. I didn't realise quite how much.'

Her hand on his was small and warm.

'You've asked a lot of yourself, Matt,' she said quietly. 'Taking on three children in a place like this—with work demands, emotional demands, your whole life changed.'

He covered her hand with his.

'What I didn't realise,' he said slowly, 'was how I would feel about the children. They were pretty much abstract to me—sure, they were my brother's children, I'd seen them a few times, I'd made a promise to him and I was going to keep that promise. It was only when I got here, when I met the children, when I began to get to know them—to become fond of them—that I really began to see what I'd taken on. This isn't just some responsibility I have to carry out. This is for life—my life, and theirs.'

It was a moment before Lesley replied.

'I know that, Matt,' she said, her voice low.

He put his hand on her chin, turning her face towards him.

'Lesley,' he said, and then he stopped, not sure what it was he wanted to say to her.

'You're right, Matt,' she said quickly. 'We do have to make sure that Christmas is still Christmas for them.'

She sat up. 'And the village trip—when were you thinking we would do that?'

He shook his head. 'We'll talk about it,' he told her, 'but not right now.'

Her lips were warm under his, and her slim body fitted against his as it always had. There was a wonderful familiarity about having her in his arms, Matt thought as he kissed her, but there was something more, something that had never been there before.

Something he had better hold in check, he realised, knowing all too well that his lips and his arms were becoming more searching, more demanding.

And, as before, there was a moment when he knew that everything in Lesley was on the point of responding to these demands. He wasn't sure which of them made the first move to draw apart, but in the moonlight she looked up at him, bewilderment in her grey eyes.

Then, as he looked at her, she recovered and smiled.

'Cool it, Doctor, dear,' she told him, and her voice was so light, so easy, that the moment was gone. 'Don't you think we should get down to some forward planning for that trip?'

'You're right, we should,' Matt agreed, and he hoped that his voice, too, was light and easy.

Perhaps they should go as soon as possible, he said, because things did seem fairly quiet at the hospital.

'You never know, of course, what will turn up, but at least we have more idea on your side. What's your population explosion like?'

Lesley held up one hand.

'Four babies due any time now, one more I have a feeling will arrive early. But they're all straightfoward and, between Agnes Cekiso and Peggy Thorpe, there shouldn't be any problem. How long will we be away, Matt?'

Two days, Matt told her, working from notes of Peter's and Clare's visits there. A few hours to reach the first of the distant villages, a few hours for his TB clinic and for Lesley's birth control talk to the women. They'd spend the night there, move on early to the other village, spend a few hours there and then back to Thabanvaba.

'I'd like to spend more time, take in a couple more

villages,' he said, regretfully, 'but we can't afford to
be away from the hospital for any longer.'

'And the children, with Christmas so close,' Lesley
reminded him.

'And the children,' he agreed.

He stood up, and drew her to her feet.

'You'd better go,' he told her. 'This is dangerous
moonlight.'

Lesley looked up at the darkness of the sky. 'But
there's no moonlight,' she said, surprised.

'I know,' Matt agreed. 'That's what's dangerous.'

She burst out laughing, and after a moment Matt
laughed, too.

'We don't laugh as much as we used to, Matt,' she
said quietly.

'No, I don't suppose we do,' Matt agreed. Her face
was no more than a dim shadow as he looked down
at her.

'Things have changed between us, haven't they,
Lesley?' he said.

And it seemed as if all the warm darkness around
closed in on them, as he waited for her to reply.

CHAPTER SIX

IT WASN'T easy to answer Matt, but Lesley knew that she had to be honest with him.

'Yes, Matt,' she said slowly, 'things have changed between us. Your life has changed because of your promise to Peter, and—you've changed. I said we don't laugh as much as we used to, and that's true. But it isn't much of a laughing matter, losing your brother and taking on his children. I know that. I accept it, but the change in you does mean that things have changed between us. It would be foolish to pretend otherwise.'

In the dim light of the stoep Matt looked down at her.

'And you're not comfortable with that change,' he said quietly.

Lesley turned her head, needing to avoid the steadiness of his eyes on her.

'I'm not sure about that,' she said with difficulty. And then, because they had always been completely honest with each other, she felt for the right words, words that would help both of them to understand, and went on, 'I like seeing you with the children. I like seeing the closeness there is between you and all three of them. But sometimes you're not the Matt I knew— sometimes you seem to be a stranger.'

Matt was quiet for a long time.

'There isn't anything I can do about that, Lesley,' he said. 'It's early days yet for me and for the children but we do laugh—we do have fun sometimes, you know. It isn't all heavy going. And it will get better.'

Lesley put her hand over his.

'I know that,' she said unevenly. 'I think you're doing a great job with them. And you're right, it is early days yet for them. And for you.' She hesitated, but it had to be said. 'It isn't only with the children, though, Matt. Other things have changed, too.'

In the warm darkness Matt sighed.

'I know what you're telling me,' he said, and suddenly, wonderfully, he was the old Matt, the Matt she knew so well. 'I do come on a bit heavy sometimes, don't I? I have absolutely no right to object if you and David Balfour fancy each other, and I know that. I'm—sorry about that, Lesley.'

The sheer relief of finding the old Matt made Lesley laugh. And made her decide that her honesty had gone far enough, and she wasn't going to say anything to Matt about how she had felt when he had kissed her and held her in that demanding and so disturbing way.

'I don't fancy David,' she assured him. 'And I don't think he fancies me—that's just his way. Maybe we should divert his attention to Anna-Marie.'

Matt shook his head.

'I think she's a bit Wagnerian for him. You know—statuesque, a bit forbidding.'

He kissed her lightly, his lips warm on hers but no more than that, and then he stood up and took both her hands in his.

'Like I said,' he reminded her, 'this is dangerous moonlight. I'll walk you home.'

Home.

The small, rather spartan room in the nurses' home. She had her photographs and some of her clothes around, but there was nothing else which made it really hers. I'll talk to Sylvia about buying a couple of rugs that the women weave, she decided.

Looking at her photographs reminded her that she had to finish an air-letter to her mother and father, ready for Ken to take when he went through to Umtata the next day for supplies for the hospital and for the mission station.

She read over what she had written, telling her folks

about the hospital, about the children and about how well Matt was doing with them.

> Not quite our over-Africa trip, but certainly a very different life from London and St Margaret's. Right now our big priority is to make Christmas as good as possible for Sarah and Colin and Jenny. We've started with the advent calendar, Sarah and Colin are working on a Christmas present for Matt and we'll have a tree.

She stopped, her pen still in her hand. Would her mother make too much out of that 'we'? Her parents had liked Matt from the start, and she knew very well that her mother had had great hopes for the over-Africa trip.

No, she couldn't change that 'we' because she was part of that Christmas scene with the children, with Matt. So Mum would just have to read whatever she wanted into it.

> Matt and I have to make a visit to a couple of the villages in the next valley. Matt will do his TB check-ups, and I'll do what I can on the contraception side. Should be interesting. It's late now, and this has to go off tomorrow. I'll write again soon.
>
> Love to you all, Lesley.

She sealed the letter and addressed it. It was strange to think of that letter leaving the mission hospital tomorrow, and a week later lying on the mat at home in Surrey.

Two days later she and Matt left before dawn in the Land Rover for the next valley, taking medical supplies and food for the journey. The noisy engine made talking impossible, but when they stopped to have coffee and sandwiches Lesley asked Matt about the TB check-ups he would do.

'It's less a check-up,' Matt said, 'than a follow-up—an attempt to get as many people as possible to realise that they must not stop taking medication when they leave hospital and when they feel better.

'The first phase of treatment kills only the active bacilli, and in normal circumstances it takes another four months to kill the disease. Half-completed treatments only kill off the weaker strains of the disease, and that leaves behind the tougher and more resistant strains. Then they need treatment which is twenty times more expensive, takes four times as long and often fails.' He smiled. 'Sorry, I didn't mean to treat you to a lecture, but that's my real job—to chase up the people we've discharged.'

He put the basket with the Thermos back in the Land Rover.

'But, of course,' he said, 'there will be other things to do. Dressings to change, a burn or two to treat, maybe some stitching to be done. I'd like your help with that, but we'll work it out when we get there.'

Two hours later they dropped into the next valley and saw the circle of thatched huts on the top of a hill.

As Matt had said, there were people waiting to see them and Lesley thought they looked as if they had been waiting patiently for some time. She and Matt had brought a portable steriliser with them, but when instruments had to be re-sterilised, ready for immediate use, Matt pointed to a large black pot sitting on the fire.

'Heavens,' Lesley said, startled, with visions of cannibal pots ready for missionaries. She could see, by the smile Matt tried to hide, that he had had the same thoughts.

They got to work, and Lesley handed Matt the instruments he needed and did the necessary bandaging. In the afternoon she got the women gathered together and, using one of the younger women as an interpreter, she talked to them about contraception—about the value of planning and spacing to their own health and to their ability to bring up children. Then she spoke to them about the need to come for regular check-ups at the hospital during pregnancy.

One of the older women said something, and Lesley asked her interpreter what she'd said.

'She say many children are needed—to work the land and to care for the parents when they grow old,' the young woman told her. 'She say her husband will want new wife if she does not give him children.'

Not easy to answer, Lesley thought ruefully.

'Tell her,' she said carefully, 'that if she has healthy children she needs fewer to work the land because they will work well. And if she herself has fewer pregnancies she will stay healthy and won't need her children to look after her.' She smiled, hoping to raise a smile or two in return. 'And tell her that if she stays healthy, and if she isn't always busy with babies, her husband won't want a new wife!'

She did get one or two smiles when her interpreter finished speaking, but none from the woman who had spoken.

'I don't think I really got through to them,' she said, telling Matt about her clinic later. 'I did get three of the younger women to agree to Depo-Provera, and they'd got their husbands to agree, too. I think that's a real breakthrough.'

'It is,' Matt agreed. 'I remember Clare saying the younger women do see that it's better to plan their families, but so often the men won't accept that.'

'I must ask Agnes Cekiso more about their customs and their traditions. Maybe that would help me to understand how to get through to them. And I'd like to be able to come here regularly,' Lesley said. 'I think in time I could get more of them to see the sense of what I'm telling them, especially if I know better where they're coming from.'

Matt's raised eyebrows at her assumption that she was going to be around long enough to do that made her flush, and she changed the subject quickly.

'We start early tomorrow morning for the next village?' she asked him.

Matt nodded.

'And these are our huts for tonight,' he told her, pointing to two round thatched huts a little apart from the others. 'I think they belong to the *sangoma*—the wise man, the medicine man—and his family. Apparently they vacate them when we come.'

They ate their evening meal with the villagers, a stew—which Matt told Lesley cheerfully was probably goat—and mealie-pap.

'Sort of like couscous,' Lesley said firmly and positively, but Matt only smiled and asked if she'd had enough or if she wanted more.

'No,' Lesley replied hastily, 'this will do.'

The clouds had been building up all afternoon, and by the time they went to their huts they could hear the rumble of distant thunder and saw jagged streaks of lightning on the distant mountains encircling the valley. Lesley, to her own surprise, fell asleep quickly, but woke in the sudden brightness of sheet lightning and a rumble of thunder directly overhead. Thunder—and then unbelievably heavy rain.

She sat up in her sleeping bag, her heart thudding. It was foolish, she knew, but she was terrified of storms. And this was a storm unlike any she had ever experienced in its sound and its ferocity.

Another clap of thunder seemed to split the sky apart and Lesley, terror engulfing her, jumped out of her sleeping bag and ran out of the open door of her hut into Matt's hut, oblivious to the torrential rain that soaked through her thin cotton nightie.

'Matt—Matt!' she said, kneeling beside the figure in the sleeping bag. 'Matt, wake up—there's the most awful storm!'

In a frightening blaze from sheet lightning she saw Matt look up at her, his eyes for a moment unfocussed.

'Lesley? Lesley, you're soaked. For heaven's sake—'

Thunder followed the lightning, and Lesley threw herself into Matt's arms, clinging to him with her face buried against him.

As the thunder died away there was silence, broken only by the steady rain on the thatched roof of the hut.

'You don't like storms?' Matt asked, and Lesley managed to recover enough to reply that that was the understatement of the year.

'You'd better stay here, then, until it's over,' he said, and Lesley thought that it would have taken a team of wild horses to make her do anything else.

In the darkness she felt his hands on the thin cotton of her shortie nightie.

'You'd better get that off—it's soaked,' he told her, and she was grateful that he showed no amusement or derision at her reaction to the storm. It was dark now, but a moment later the beam of a torch cut through the darkness. 'Here's a towel,' Matt said. 'Dry yourself. The only thing I can offer you is this T-shirt.'

She had just pulled the T-shirt on when there was another blaze of lightning. Immediately Matt's arms were around her, holding her close before the deafening clap of thunder followed.

'Right overhead, I'd say,' he murmured. He didn't let her go.

'I didn't know you felt like this about storms,' he said, conversationally, and Lesley knew that he was trying to help her back to normality.

'I don't usually feel this bad,' she told him, and now, with his arms around her, she could keep her voice steady. 'But I've never in my life heard or seen a storm like this!'

'It should begin to pass over now,' Matt said, and

when the world lit up again and the thunder rolled she shut her eyes and clung to him.

'That was longer, that time, between the lightning and the thunder, wasn't it?' Matt said. 'And the thunder wasn't quite as bad.'

Lesley wasn't sure, afterwards, just when her fear of the storm was taken over by a realisation of Matt's body close to hers in the darkness of the hut. Her heart was thudding unevenly—or was it his? She didn't know, and it didn't matter as his lips found hers. This time there was no fighting the urgent demand of his lips, his hands, and the equally urgent response of her own body.

She didn't know, either, when the storm finally passed over, but there was no more than the faint distant rumble of thunder when she and Matt drew apart.

In the darkness she felt Matt's finger trace the curve of her cheek and rest on her lips.

'You know what?' he murmured. 'I think we've been doing too much talking, and not enough of this.'

'You may be right,' Lesley replied, not quite steadily, 'but there hasn't been much opportunity.'

'I know that,' Matt said with feeling. 'I know it very well.'

The darkness was beginning to lift, and she could see him leaning on his elbow, looking down at her.

'Much as I'd like to have you stay here,' he murmured, 'maybe you'd better go back to your own hut.' There was warm laughter in his voice now. 'You can keep my T-shirt—it's just long enough to be decent, and fortunately your hut is right next to mine.'

'Very fortunately,' Lesley agreed feelingly, remembering her frightened rush across in the storm.

She felt his hand touch her hair.

'I'm glad you haven't had time to get it cut,' he said. And then added, 'See you later, Sister.' His lips brushed hers in a brief and warm reminder of the hours in each other's arms.

'Anything you say, Doctor, dear,' Lesley returned.

There was no one around as she ran back to her own hut, but she could see the first rosy streaks of dawn in the east. She washed in the basin of water which one of the women had carried to the hut for her the night before, and put her uniform on, pinning her hair up. If I do this for work I could keep it longer, she thought.

They had coffee and bread for breakfast, and left for the more distant village to get at least some of their journey done before the real heat of the day. It was mid-morning before they drew up in the centre of the circle of huts to see, as there had been yesterday, a patient group of waiting people.

As Matt had expected, there were two people with burns—one an old man and the other a young woman. Lesley cleaned the young woman's arm and the old man's leg, and put on the gauze dressings they had brought with them, followed by bandages.

'And next week someone must bring you to the hospital so that we can change the dressings,' Matt said sternly. 'Next time, even if it's difficult, you must come right away.'

Neither of the burns was infected, fortunately, but Lesley knew that so often by the time the villagers came to the hospital the burn wounds were infected.

'I tell them, but I know it's difficult for people so far away to come,' Matt said, when he had finished his TB check-ups and Lesley had talked to the women. 'Peter said it was one of the frustrating things about his work here, knowing that he was so often asking the impossible of the villagers. But we'll keep on trying.'

It was late afternoon when they finished, and part of their journey back to Thabanvaba would be in the dark. The roads weren't too good, and Lesley was certain that Matt, like herself, must be thinking of Peter and Clare and the accident that had cost them their lives.

Just let us get as far as possible before it's dark, Lesley thought with a silent prayer. But one moment it

was still daylight, although the sun had gone down
behind the distant purple hills, and then, with startling
swiftness, it was night. Since coming to Thabanvaba,
she had often thought that the warm African night was
so different from the nights she had known. And different—driving along in the dark, miles from anywhere—
to night in the hospital in the settlement.

Suddenly Matt drew up.

'I'm bushed,' he said, and Lesley, looking at him,
saw how exhausted he looked. 'I need to have a rest
before I drive on.'

'Couldn't I drive?' Lesley asked, but he shook
his head.

'Not in conditions like this,' he replied. 'The Land
Rover's heavy, and it isn't easy to drive. I think it could
be a good idea for you to be able to drive it, but not
right now. No, I'll stretch out for half an hour, then I'll
be fine.'

He unrolled one sleeping bag in the back of the Land
Rover, and used the other as a pillow.

'Can't take more than half an hour,' he said, 'but
that will be fine. Can you stay awake, Lesley, and wake
me? You must be pretty tired, too.'

'I'm all right,' Lesley said, not quite truthfully. 'I'll
stay awake.'

Matt was asleep almost instantly.

The storm of the night before had cleared the threatening clouds and the moon, almost full, shone clearly.
In its light, Lesley looked down at Matt's sleeping face,
the dark lashes resting on his cheeks and his dark hair
rumpled.

He looked younger and defenceless asleep, she
thought, and there was a strange feeling somewhere
inside her, a feeling she didn't want to look into too
deeply. Colin looked very like this when he was asleep,
apart from the endearing freckles on his small nose.

There was still some coffee in the Thermos, as well
as some sandwiches, and she moved away from Matt's

side and set out the two mugs, ready to pour coffee for them to have before this last stretch of the journey.

Matt was fast asleep, but the half-hour was up and Lesley leaned over him. Gently, she touched his cheek with one finger.

'Matt,' she said, 'it's time to wake up.'

All the years of being on call made him react immediately. He opened his eyes, and looked up at her.

'There's coffee before we move on,' Lesley said.

He sat up then, and took both her hands in his.

'Lesley,' he said, 'will you marry me?'

CHAPTER SEVEN

'WILL you marry me?' Matt said again, when Lesley didn't reply.

Once—a long time ago, it seemed to her—she would have laughed, and she would have told him that it would serve him right if she took him seriously and accepted him.

Now—now she couldn't do that.

'Oh, Matt,' she said at last, not quite steadily. 'I wish you hadn't asked me.'

His eyes were very dark.

'I thought you might say that,' he said, 'but I had to. I—thought you might have known that I would.'

I did know, Lesley thought, somewhere deep inside. I think I have known for a little while. But I didn't want to face up to it. And now I have to.

She wished now that she had admitted to herself that Matt would ask her to marry him because, if she had, she would have been prepared—she would have known what to say, how to reply to him.

'We said right from the start that marriage wasn't in our plans,' she said slowly, searching for the right words. She remembered saying to Brenda once that even when she did come to think of marriage she didn't think it would be to Matt, and that suited both of them very well.

'Things have changed,' Matt said quietly. 'Everything has changed.'

Afterwards, Lesley was to wish she had said nothing more—to wish she had just kept quiet then.

'Matt,' she said, knowing she sounded a little desperate, 'I'm very fond of the children—I love them, but I just don't know that I could take on a ready-made family.'

His hands, holding both of hers, let go. Not suddenly, but quite slowly.

'You think this is because of the children,' he said flatly, and it wasn't a question.

I shouldn't have said that, Lesley thought, but it was too late.

'I didn't mean—' she began, but his lean, unsmiling face stopped her. 'Matt, I meant it when I said that sometimes I feel as if I don't know you—as if you're a stranger,' she said, wanting to make him understand. 'Maybe you're right—maybe we do need to get to know each other all over again. Maybe I need time to do that, to get to know you again.'

He climbed out of the back of the Land Rover and stood still as she scrambled out to stand beside him.

'For the record,' he said, very quietly, 'from the moment I left you in London I missed you. After you came to Thabanvaba I was so darned glad to be with you again, and I began to see how blind I had been, not realising that I wanted to spend the rest of my life with you. And last night, holding you in my arms, made me completely certain that I had to ask you to marry me. I'm sorry about that, Lesley. I can't say let's forget I said it because I can't—and I don't suppose you can—but we'll put it behind us, and I won't say it again.'

He unscrewed the Thermos, and poured coffee into the mugs she had set out ready.

'Let's have our coffee and get on,' he said. 'Fortunately the moonlight helps—this last stretch shouldn't be too bad.'

'Matt. . .' Lesley began unsteadily.

He smiled, but it was a smile that didn't reach his eyes.

'Do me a favour, Lesley, don't say any more,' he said lightly, easily. 'Except this. I hope we can agree that this won't make any difference to working together, or to Christmas?'

Lesley lifted her chin.

'You didn't need to say that, Matt,' she told him. 'It goes without saying that nothing personal will affect our working together. And I'm as determined as you are that Christmas will be as good as we can possibly make it for the children.'

She finished her coffee, and when Matt had finished his she took both mugs and the Thermos and put them back in the basket. And for the rest of the journey she was very glad that the noise of the Land Rover made talking impossible.

It was midnight when Matt drew up inside the hospital compound, and Sam Ngewe closed and locked the gate behind them.

'We won't unpack tonight,' Matt said. 'We both need to get some sleep. Thanks for coming, Lesley—I think we achieved something.'

His voice was easy, friendly, as was the nod he gave her as he headed for the house at the far side and she turned towards the door to the nurses' home. As she closed the door she looked back. Matt was just closing the gate behind him and somehow his careful, deliberate action dismayed and distressed her. As if he's shutting a door on what happened, she thought, as if he's shutting me out.

Don't be ridiculous, she told herself firmly in her room. I'm the one who did the shutting out. And of course I had to say no.

But not the way I did it.

She should have put it another way, she realised, and she wished that she had. She hadn't really meant that he was asking her because of the children. And yet it was true that she felt she wasn't ready to take on three children, just like that. She would have to be very, very sure of what she was doing to agree to that.

But it wasn't only because of the children that she

had said no. The rest of it was true, too—that she did feel sometimes that she didn't know this Matt, that he was a stranger.

And yet—

And yet, she admitted with some reluctance, a stranger whose arms she had slept in, a stranger whose very touch could make everything in her respond to him.

In spite of her weariness after the tiring hours of the journey, it was a long time before she got to sleep. She was grateful that the maternity ward was quiet the next day—so quiet that when Sylvia Fraser came in to visit one of the new mothers and her baby Lesley could agree to leave young Faith in charge for ten minutes.

'I brought a few of the rugs you were interested in,' Sylvia said. 'We could see how they look in your room.'

Lesley had mentioned to her that she would like to brighten up her room with some of the hand-woven rugs. Now, seeing one in soft greens and blues and another in autumn colours, she found it difficult to decide which she liked best.

'I think the bluey-green one,' she said at last. 'But I'd need two—one beside the bed and the other at the dressing-table. Pity about the curtains—they don't go too well, but the rugs will make such a difference.'

'I like your choice,' Sylvia said. 'I always think that sort of cool colour makes the heat more bearable. I think there's another rug the same in stock and, if you don't mind waiting a week or two, we could do you curtains to match.'

Curtains, and the two rugs—it was ridiculous to feel that anything like that was committing her to staying longer at Thabanvaba than she meant to, Lesley told herself. Because when she did go she could easily just take them with her.

'Thanks, Sylvia, I'd like that,' she said firmly.

Was it her imagination, she wondered, or did Sylvia look thinner and were her eyes more shadowed?

'How are things with you, Sylvia?' she asked.

The older woman smiled.

'This isn't one of my best days,' she admitted, and Lesley knew she hadn't imagined the pain behind the shadows under Sylvia's eyes. 'But I've started this new treatment—Dr Lunn in Umtata managed to get enough for three of his cancer patients, and I'm on his experimental programme. Ken brought my cocktail of drugs back with him. I've only had two days so I can't expect miracles this soon.' And then, her smile gone, she said with difficulty, 'I don't expect miracles, really, Lesley, just a little longer than they seem to think I have. For Ken, for the children and for myself. So, yes, maybe just a small miracle.'

Lesley put her hand over Sylvia's.

'You deserve your small miracle, Sylvia,' she said, not quite steadily. 'Are your children coming home for Christmas? I'm looking forward to meeting them.'

Sylvia shook her head.

'They have done since they started going to boarding school,' she said. 'But this year they both have the chance of a school trip to Austria—a skiiing holiday. Ken and I couldn't afford it, but my parents and Ken's father have clubbed together. I didn't want them to miss the chance, although I would have liked to have them home this Christmas.'

For a moment her eyes met Lesley's, and the words were there, unspoken—perhaps this last Christmas. Then Sylvia lifted her chin.

'Next Christmas,' she said very steadily, 'they'll be home. I'd particularly like our Julie to meet you—she wants to do nursing.'

She stood up.

'That's, of course, if you're still here at Thabanvaba,' she said, a question in her voice.

They walked to the door together.

'I don't know about that,' Lesley said honestly. 'I can't quite think that far ahead right now.'

Sylvia nodded.

'I can understand that,' she said. She hesitated, and then said, slowly, 'Take your time, Lesley. Don't let yourself be rushed into anything, one way or the other. Give it all time.'

Lesley made her way back to the ward, thinking about this. And more than ever wishing she had given Matt an answer differently. Wishing she could take back what she had said.

At least I know where I stand, Matt told himself. And at least I didn't—in the words of the old song—at least I didn't 'spoil it all by saying something stupid like I love you'.

Although, perhaps, he should have said that right at the start to get that straight up front. Perhaps if he had, Lesley wouldn't have thought he wanted to marry her because of the children.

All right, it was asking a lot of her to take on the children, a ready-made family, but he had seen her with each one of them and he had seen their growing closeness.

And he had thought—foolishly, he saw now—that she wouldn't be put off by the package deal, the deal that included the children. He had got it the wrong way round, of course, he saw that now. He had seen the two of them, Lesley and himself, as the principals in the marriage thing. He had thought that marriage, once so far from both their minds, would be wonderful—the only thing he wanted now with things so changed between them. With the package deal that included the children as part of that.

Instead, Lesley saw it the other way round. She thought he wanted to marry her because of the children, because of sharing the responsibility and the caring for them. Because it was a good and a sensible idea.

But how could she think that after those hours in each other's arms in the storm? How in all the world could she think that?

It had hurt, it had hurt damnably and it went on hurting. But he wasn't going to let Lesley see that.

In the hospital it was no problem. They were accustomed, both of them, to separating their private and their professional lives. But, at the same time, Matt had to admit that the closeness and the warmth between them had made a shared glance, an unspoken understanding, lend an extra dimension to working together. A dimension that had gone now.

The times when they were together with the children, were more difficult. The first night after their village trip Lesley came over, as usual, as soon as she came off duty. Matt himself was a little later finishing, and she was sitting on the stoep with Sarah and Colin when he got home. Jenny was already in bed, Sarah told him, and she wanted Uncle Matt to say goodnight to her.

'She's prob'ly sleeping,' Colin told him. 'Isn't it a good thing we did the little window at lunchtime? Patience said she needed a good early night, especially if we're going to go to Umtata tomorrow.'

Matt shook his head.

'Not tomorrow,' he said firmly. 'I have an appendectomy and a hernia booked, never mind what comes up without being booked. What about the day after? How are you for that, Lesley?'

Lesley thought about it.

'All right, now that Peggy Thorpe is here,' she said. 'We're actually fairly reasonable right now.'

'And it's getting awfully close to Christmas,' Colin pointed out.

When Matt came back from saying goodnight to a very sleepy little girl Patience, with the children helping, had brought a meat loaf and a big bowl of salad out to the table on the stoep. Sarah and Colin talked about the trip to Umtata, and Matt, although he wished now he had never agreed to it, began to feel that the sooner it was done the better.

'We'd better get up in the middle of the night,' Colin

suggested, 'so that we have plenty of time there.'

'He doesn't really mean the middle of the night,' Sarah said anxiously, 'just very early in the morning.'

'I do mean the middle of the night,' Colin returned, his lower lip sticking out pugnaciously. 'I do *so*, Sarah!'

'It takes about three hours, doesn't it?' Lesley said quickly. 'Maybe we should leave just as soon as it's light, and ask Patience to pack us something to eat on the way.'

The discussions of the trip lasted throughout supper, and after that it was time for baths and then bed for Sarah and Colin.

'I think I'll go off now, Matt, and have an early night,' Lesley said, when they had said goodnight to the children. 'I'm sure you can do with an early night, too.'

'That's a good idea,' Matt replied, and he wasn't sure whether he felt disappointed or relieved at Lesley's going so soon.

Disappointed, he admitted an hour later as he sat alone in the warm darkness. But perhaps it was better than the two of them sitting here together, awkward and ill-at-ease, neither of them knowing what to say.

Because he was pretty sure that's how it would have been. Oh, they had agreed to put it behind them—what he had said, what Lesley had replied—but it wouldn't be easy, especially not at first.

And the following evening, because of the long trip to Umtata and back, an early night made sense, too, and Lesley left as soon as Sarah and Colin were in bed.

'Sure you can cope?' Matt asked David Balfour when the young doctor came out to say goodbye to them at first light the next morning.

'No problem,' David assured him airily. 'Just as long as no one needs an emergency op today I'll do fine. Wish I was coming with you, though. Makes a nice change, seeing you out of uniform, Lesley.'

His grey eyes took in, with obvious admiration, Lesley's pink cotton dress, her long brown legs in sandals and her fair curly hair, tied back from her face.

'Have a nice day, kids,' he said then. 'Pretty Alice-band, Sarah. I like your hair that way.'

Sarah's cheeks were pink with pleasure. Lesley is right, it's just his way, Matt thought—little girls, big girls. Easy, uncomplicated. No wonder Lesley is smiling at him like that.

'See you tomorrow, David,' he said, hoping he didn't sound as brusque as he felt. 'Good luck.'

He hadn't thought of the long journey to Umtata—three hours of sitting still, confined in a small space—and when Colin asked for the third time if they were nearly there, he replied, more sharply than he meant to, that it was only ten minutes since he had said, no, they weren't nearly there.

'I think we should play I Spy,' Lesley said. 'We always used to on long car journeys to pass the time. Sarah, you can start.'

By the time they had given in on S-W-N, which turned out to be Sociable Weavers' Nests, and guessed H-O-G, which was Herd of Goats, and stuck on one or two others it was time to hand round the rolls and the fruit juice for breakfast. Lesley had Jenny strapped in beside her in the front so that she could supervise the eating and drinking, and soon after that Jenny fell asleep and slept until they were almost at Umtata.

'We could sing Christmas carols,' Sarah suggested, a little diffidently. 'We did that last year when we went to Durban.'

For a moment Matt found Lesley's eyes meeting his, and for the first time in these last few days there was no guarded reserve between them.

'That's a good idea,' she said, and she eased the sleeping child into a more comfortable position. 'But let's sing softly—we don't want to wake Jenny.'

They sang all the familiar Christmas carols, Lesley's sweet and surprisingly strong voice leading. Matt remembered last Christmas, in the small stone church

near her home in Surrey, and the same carols. He wondered if Lesley was remembering that, too—and
remembering how easy and casual things had been
between them then.

Umtata was hot and dusty and crowded. The shops
were bright and busy, with Christmas less than a fortnight away, but—as Ken Fraser had said—there wasn't
much in the way of toy shops for the children to see.

'What about that department store?' Lesley suggested. 'There must be a toy department there.'

Matt was carrying Jenny because of the crowds, and
Lesley had Sarah's hand on one side, and Colin's on
the other, firmly in hers.

'It's a good one,' Colin said. 'Look what it's called—
OK Bazaar! So it has to be OK!'

Overcome by his own wit, he doubled over in laughter. Lesley's eyes met Matt's, and for a moment
everything was as it had been before. Open and warm
and easy. But only for a moment before the reserve
returned to Lesley's face.

'Let's see if we can find where the toys are,' she
said brightly.

The toy department was on the first floor, and Colin
right away found a fire-engine that made loud noises—
with a ladder that could zoom up and down. Then he
decided that a tractor with a trailer and a forklift was
even better.

'Look, Uncle Matt. I see doggie, I see Murray,' Jenny
said excitedly. A young man was showing a few different battery-operated toys, and the one that Jenny had
seen was a golden dog with ears like Murray's, alert
and pointed. As they watched the dog moved over the
floor, did somersaults, turned in cricles and then began
to slow down.

'Again—do it again,' Jenny said delightedly, clap-
ping her hands.

Matt put her down, and she joined the other children
standing watching, entranced.

Sarah was walking round the dolls—slowly—and for a moment Matt and Lesley were on their own.

'Matt, have you thought how we're going to go about this present business?' Lesley asked and, in spite of everything, his heart lifted at that 'we'.

'Ken will be back here next week,' he told her. 'I thought if the children do these letters and we see what it is they want then Ken could get them for us. He says he'll be glad to do it.'

Lesley was looking at Jenny.

'I don't think there's much doubt about what Jenny wants,' she said. 'But Colin wants everything he sees.'

'He'll have to learn that he can't have everything he wants,' Matt said, tersely. 'That's life.' The moment he had said it he was ashamed of himself.

Lesley's grey eyes darkened, but she didn't say anything. And Matt, desperately wishing he hadn't said it, couldn't manage to say any more—to say that he was sorry.

'Doggy tired,' Jenny said, turning back to them. 'Sleeping now.'

'We'll have to have plenty of batteries,' Lesley murmured, and the lift of her chin and the warm colour in her cheeks made him even more ashamed of what he had said.

'I think we need to think about lunch,' he said as Colin and Sarah came back to them, Colin talking excitedly about a racing-car track. 'What should we have for lunch?'

For a moment the little boy's exuberance faded.

'You tell them, Sarah,' he said uncertainly. 'Tell them what we do.'

'We always have hamburgers and Coke,' Sarah said, and added anxiously, 'but we don't have to this time.'

'I think that sounds a perfect lunch,' Lesley said steadily. 'Don't you, Matt?'

'I can't think of anything better,' Matt agreed.

And now—in their shared concern for the children,

for the memories that must be hurting—there was no barrier, no constraint. There were unshed tears behind Lesley's grey eyes, Matt saw.

'It's all right, Lesley,' he said softly. 'We'll make it all right.'

She smiled.

'Yes, we will,' she replied, just as softly.

And he knew that, like him, she was sure that no matter how things were between the two of them, nothing would change their determination to make Christmas as 'all right' as possible for the children.

CHAPTER EIGHT

WE'LL make it work, Lesley told herself determinedly. We have to, for the children.

She wished with all her heart that she could do something or say something to put things right between Matt and herself, but that was not going to be easily done. Sometimes his guard would drop—or hers would—and there would be a moment when the old warmth, the old closeness, was there. But it would be no more than a fleeting moment before that curtain between them was there again.

Lunchtime, with the hamburgers and the Coke which seemed to be part of this Christmas outing, was noisy and the restaurant on the top floor of the department store was crowded. Lesley wasn't sorry about that because it made any strain between Matt and her less noticeable.

'I think I'll have tea instead of Coke,' she said, and Matt said he would join her.

'That's all right,' Colin assured them, 'that's what Mummy and Daddy always did. Mummy doesn't like Coke.'

And then, in a small voice, he said, 'I mean, Mummy didn't like Coke.'

For a moment, an unguarded moment, Lesley's eyes met Matt's. Sarah's hand, holding her Coke, was still— her brown eyes anguished.

'I remember your mummy not liking Coke, Colin,' Matt said gently. 'But surely your daddy did?'

Colin nodded.

'Yes, Daddy liked Coke, but not with hamburgers.'

'I bet he liked tomato sauce, though,' Matt said. He lifted up the small plastic sachet of tomato sauce. 'Once, when I was about your age, Sarah, our gran took us out and we had hamburgers. Your dad liked the tomato sauce so much that he took one of these things with him. We were walking through a big shop much like this one, and your dad must have squeezed the tomato sauce because it jumped out all over a lady who was passing.'

'Was it all over her clothes?' Colin asked, fascinated.

Matt nodded.

'And her face, and her hair.'

Even Sarah was smiling now. That was just the right thing to say, Matt, Lesley thought, and across the table she hoped that her eyes told him so.

''Mato sauce,' Jenny said, smiling widely at them all.

'That's good, Jenny—say it again,' Colin said, and Jenny obliged.

'Jenny's talking so well now,' Sarah commented, and again Lesley felt that constriction in her throat at the grown-up, responsible air of the nine-year-old. 'Colin was much slower. I think he was almost three before anyone but me could understand what he was saying.'

'I was not slow,' Colin said, outraged. 'I was very good, Sarah, much better than Jenny.'

''Mato sauce,' Jenny said again loudly, and the delight on her small face at this success made them all laugh—even Colin, after a moment's reluctance.

'Is there anything else we should do on this trip?' Matt asked then. 'Remember, we won't be away from Thabanvaba again before Christmas.'

Sarah and Colin looked at each other.

'There's a Father Christmas here—in that place called the Fairy Grotto, where the toys are. It's a little bit different from where Father Christmas is when we go to Cape Town or to Durban,' Colin said. 'Children go and they sit on his knee and they tell him what they want for Christmas.'

'Is that what you do next?' Lesley asked.

'We don't actually go and speak to him,' Sarah said,

'but—but there's a wishing well, and you get lucky packets there and we usually get them and we open them in the car.'

Matt stood up and scooped Jenny into his arms.

'Then that's what we'll do,' he said. 'Sure you don't want to sit on Father Christmas's knee?'

'It's just one of his helpers,' Colin explained. 'The real Father Christmas is much too busy to go round all the toy shops, you see, Uncle Matt.'

'Of course,' Matt replied gravely. 'I should have thought of that.'

Five minutes later three children clutched large bright cardboard lucky packets.

'Let's go back to the car right now,' Colin said impatiently, 'so's we can open them.'

'Bathroom trip first,' Lesley said firmly. 'Boys one floor up, girls this floor—meet at the main door, Matt?'

'Yes, ma'am,' Matt replied, and he saluted. 'Come on, Colin, we've got our orders. Do what the Boss Lady says.'

Lesley was still smiling when she took Sarah and Jenny along to the cloakroom.

'I like it when Uncle Matt's funny,' Sarah said.

'So do I, Sarah,' Lesley agreed. 'So do I.'

The opening of the lucky packets, and the careful examining of the contents, made the first hour in the car pass painlessly. Jenny had been strapped into her seat in the back of the Land Rover beside Colin and Sarah, but when she began rubbing her eyes Matt drew up so that Lesley could take her on her knee. She fell asleep very quickly in Lesley's arms, both of them strapped in together, and soon after that so did Colin and Sarah.

'Good thought you had, bringing their pillows,' Matt said softly.

Lesley glanced back. 'They look like little angels asleep,' she murmured. 'Even Colin.'

Matt looked in the mirror. 'Even Colin,' he agreed.

'The lucky packets were a great success. Who would have thought that cheap plastic toys could give them so much pleasure?'

They talked then about the shopping trip, their voices low although all three children were sound asleep. The last hour before they reached Thabanvaba was in darkness, and Lesley thought it was as if the five of them were in a small enclosed world of their own, driving steadily through the night.

The warm sweet weight of the sleeping child in her arms, and an occasional glance at the other two, also asleep, gave her a strange feeling. The three sleeping children, and the two of them—Matt and herself—in this small private world.

How can I have the reservations that I do have? she wondered, troubled. How can I hold back? I've become so fond of the children, and I do think they're fond of me. It could work.

But she remembered what Sylvia had said. Take your time. Don't let yourself be rushed into anything.

And it wasn't just the children. It wasn't just the thought of taking on a ready-made family. Perhaps, Lesley thought, I could take that in my stride if I was more sure about us, about Matt and me.

In the warm darkness Matt turned his head.

'Are you asleep?' he said.

'No, I'm not. Are you?' Lesley returned, and he laughed.

And then, the laughter gone, he said, 'Lesley, I'm sorry I—said what I did, and spoiled things between us.'

'I'm sorry, too, Matt,' Lesley said. 'Sorry I answered the way I did.' She hesitated, but only for a moment, and then she said carefully, 'But that doesn't have to spoil things, Matt. Not unless we allow it to.'

She wasn't sure whether he would have said any more, or whether she would have, but Sarah woke at that moment, asking sleepily if they were nearly home.

And perhaps it was just as well, Lesley thought later, for there wasn't a great deal more to be said.

And there was no doubt that even these few words had helped. Not in making everything as it had been before between Matt and her, but—better, she thought gratefully, than those awful few days of that distance between them.

The following evening the children wrote their letters to Father Christmas just before they went to bed.

'I've done Jenny's letter for her,' Sarah explained. 'I held her hand so that she could make a sort of a J at the end.'

'Can I see?' Lesley asked.

'Oh, no,' Colin said, shocked. 'Nobody gets to see them except Father Christmas. We fold them up, and we leave them here on the table with the milk and the biscuits, and Father Christmas comes and takes them, and in the morning. . .' he paused impressively '. . .they're gone!'

For a moment Sarah's brown eyes met Lesley's, an unspoken question in them.

Do you know what you have to do?

Lesley nodded, a nod which she hoped Sarah understood.

'Sarah, how do you spell tractor?' Colin asked. 'It's the only word I can't spell. No, I want to write it myself—just tell me the letters.'

When the letters were finished, and the lights turned out in the children's rooms, Lesley and Matt came back to the lounge.

'What happens now?' Matt asked.

'You drink the milk, and you eat at least some of the biscuits,' Lesley told him.

Obediently, he did that.

'A few artistic crumbs,' he said, 'and a half-finished biscuit. How do you like that touch? As if Father Christmas just didn't have time before his next call.'

'I like it,' Lesley assured him, and she thought, And

I like that we can talk like this, you and I, without that awful distance between us.

'And now we read the letters,' she said, 'and after that we get rid of them.'

Jenny's letter was simple. 'My little sister is only two, she can't write, but she would like to have that little dog that does tricks,' Sarah had written.

Colin's letter was written in large, rather wobbly letters.

'Dear Father Crismas, I like a lot of toys, but the toy I like best is the tractor what has a traler and a foklif with it. Thank you, love, Colin.'

'Great confidence in his spelling, other than tractor,' Matt commented, smiling. 'That's nice and easy, I can tell Ken exactly what to get. Now, what about Sarah?'

Sarah's writing was neat and careful.

'Dear Father Christmas, I did not see what I want, the shop didn't have any, and if you can't get it it's all right, but if you can, what I would really like is a Bride Doll. Love from Sarah.'

Lesley and Matt looked at each other.

'There weren't any bride dolls?' Matt asked, and Lesley shook her head.

'I looked at the dolls with Sarah,' she confirmed.

Matt sighed. 'She'll be disappointed,' he said. 'I suppose we should get another kind of doll?'

'No, Matt,' Lesley said slowly. 'She wants a bride doll. I'll talk to Sylvia, Surely we can think of something. Maybe I can get hold of a doll and make it into an acceptable bride.'

'Can you do that?' Matt asked.

'I'm not sure,' Lesley admitted. 'Sewing isn't my best thing, but I can try. I'd hate Sarah to be disappointed.'

He looked at her, his eyes very dark.

'I like it when you say things like that,' he said, his voice low.

He put the letters down on the table, and sat down on the couch beside her. Then, with decided purpose,

he took her in his arms and kissed her. Gently at first—
gently, warmly. And then not at all gently, and Lesley
was very conscious of her heart thudding unevenly as
his kiss became more searching, more demanding.

It was a long time before he let her go, and when he
did he looked down at her with a question in his eyes.
A question that Lesley knew she couldn't answer. Not
now. Not yet.

And because she couldn't she saw the growing disappointment, the determined effort he made to distance
himself from her—physically and emotionally.

'Matt—' she began uncertainly, but he stopped her
with a gentle finger on her lips.

'Don't say anything,' he said, and the determined
lightness of his voice brought back the ache of sadness
to her. 'Now, let's make sure we get these letters out
of sight.'

There was nothing more she could say.

They agreed that Lesley would take the letters
back with her and put them in the hospital furnace,
and Matt wrote, in a carefully disguised hand, 'Thank
you, children—we'll see what we can do—Father
Christmas.'

'How does that look?' he asked, and Lesley assured
him that it would convince anyone.

He walked across the compound with her, talking
lightly about the hospital, about the prenatal clinic for
the next day and about the difference it had made to
all of them having David Balfour and Peggy Thorpe
here. At the door he kissed her lightly, a friendly kiss.
A kiss that said it was all right, they were friends again.

I'm very glad of that, Lesley told herself, and she
was. But she couldn't help wondering why, if she was
so glad they could go back to that easy, friendly and
undemanding stage, she kept thinking of the way she
had felt in Matt's arms—of the immediate and urgent
response of her body to his.

*   *   *

The next morning, when Lesley had just finished breakfast, one of the women who worked in the kitchen told her, giggling, that there was someone waiting to see her.

Lesley followed her through to the kitchen to find Colin, in his Mickey Mouse pyjamas, hiding under the table.

'Shh,' he said, his finger to his lips. 'I don't want Uncle Matt to know I'm here. He said we'd have to wait to tell you later, but I knew you would want to know.'

Lesley knelt down on the floor beside him.

'To know what?' she asked, knowing very well what he wanted to tell her.

'He came,' Colin said. 'He drank the milk, and he ate almost all the biscuits, and he took our letters! And you know what, Lesley? He writed a letter himself to say thank you. So—so I think that will be all right.'

'I think it will,' Lesley agreed, managing to remain as serious as the small boy himself. 'Thanks for telling me, Colin. Maybe you'd better get back home now. Are you and Sarah and Jenny going to Sylvia's playgroup now?'

In the holidays Sylvia organised the children of the hospital and mission staff into a small playgroup, which she held in her own home. Lesley had been very relieved when Matt had told her about this. Patience was wonderful with the children but they did need something more organised, especially now.

'I better hurry,' Colin said. 'And if Uncle Matt tells you that he came just pretend you don't know.'

'I'll do that,' Lesley promised, but half an hour later, when Matt looked in on her ward, he told her that he had caught Colin as he scuttled back.

'He told me you were very pleased to know,' he said, and Lesley assured him that she had been.

A little later she saw Sylvia crossing the compound, and hurried out to catch her and tell her about Sarah's request for a bride doll.

'I do have some dolls of Julie's,' Sylvia said doubtfully. 'No bride doll, but we can have a look at them. No, Julie wouldn't mind at all—she loves Sarah. Tell you what, I'll see what I can find—come over to the house in your lunch break. The children have a quiet time then, and I can slip out for five minutes.'

There were three dolls laid out in what was clearly a teenager's room when Lesley went across the compound later.

'This one,' Lesley said instantly, and she picked up the one with long flaxen hair. 'She'll make a lovely bride.'

'There's this old petticoat of mine,' Sylvia said. 'Broderie anglaise, but with this net curtain for a veil it could look right.' She looked at Lesley doubtfully. 'I wish I could say I'll do it, Lesley, but I'm tied up with the children all day, and—I'm not much use in the evenings right now.'

'How is your new treatment going?' Lesley asked, concerned.

Sylvia hesitated.

'I'm a born optimist,' she said after a moment, 'but I do think I feel better than I did. It's early days, I know that, but—I'm hoping.'

'So am I, Sylvia,' Lesley said, and she hugged the older woman. 'And I really want to do the doll for Sarah. I might ask you for advice, but I do want to do it.'

She looked at her watch.

'Clinic today, I must go. Thanks so much, Sylvia.'

She felt more comfortable with her clinic now, and she sensed that the women were more comfortable with her as she did the routine check-ups, filling in each chart.

'You're thirty-four weeks, I see, Mrs Woods,' she said to the young wife of Ken's assistant at the mission. She looked at the chart. 'Your baby was in breech position, of course, and we're hoping he's decided to change.'

'It feels as if he has—there's plenty of movement,'

Jean Woods said hopefully. But the baby was still in breech position.

'I think we'll get Dr Turner to have a look at you,' Lesley said. 'He may decide to turn your baby over—this is the right stage for that.'

Jean Woods nodded but her blue eyes were anxious.

'He did say last time he might have to try that,' she said.

'Faith, go over and ask Dr Turner if he can come, please,' Lesley asked her young assistant.

But five minutes later Faith was back with David Balfour.

'Dr Turner is busy with a kid with a burned leg,' he explained. 'Can I do anything?'

Lesley handed him her patient's chart, and told him of the baby's breech position.

'Thirty-four weeks,' he murmured as he examined the patient. He looked at Lesley. 'Best time, of course, Sister. Now, Mrs Woods, just relax. I think this little fellow is going to co-operate with us.'

Lesley had seen external versions done before, and she was happy with the skill of the young doctor's hands as they moved expertly and surely.

'There we are,' he said. He patted Jean Woods's abdomen. 'Now you just stay that way for a couple of weeks more, Baby Woods.'

When the young woman had gone the doctor turned back to Lesley.

'You know, of course, Sister, the risks of external version—rupture of the membranes, placental separation—but these dangers are less frequent than the actual dangers of breech delivery. I think she'll do nicely, and fortunately she's right here on the spot if the baby is stubborn and we do have a breech presentation.'

'Thanks, Dr Balfour,' Lesley said. 'I enjoyed seeing you do that.'

David Balfour looked at his watch.

'I think I'm off duty,' he said. 'So—do I deserve a cup of coffee, Lesley?'

'You do indeed, David,' Lesley replied, returning his easy and open smile.

Over coffee, he told her about his student days in Cape Town, and the obstetrics experiences he had had in the townships. Lesley listened, fascinated, asking questions about the system.

'Oh, yes,' he said, 'the women come in to the Midwives' Obstetric Units, they have their babies and a few hours later they go home. A week later they bring the babies back for a paediatric check-up. It isn't ideal, but it works.'

He stood up.

'Any time you need me, just send for me,' he said. 'I mean off-duty, too, of course. As long as I'm not treading on Matt's toes, I don't do that, especially to my boss!'

'Thanks for the offer, David,' Lesley said, smiling.

'Thanks but no, thanks?' David asked. He patted her hand. 'Well, remember I'm around if you change your mind.'

When he had gone she finished putting away the charts and clearing up the small clinic room, and she found herself thinking that that was how it used to be with Matt and her. Easy, uncomplicated, undemanding. And she had thought it would go on being like that for Matt and her.

But it isn't only Matt who has changed, she thought. I have changed, too.

What we had before was certainly easy and casual, but that was all. There wasn't any depth to it.

For the first time she wondered if she really did want to go back to the way things had been for Matt and her.

It was a new thought, and a disturbing one.

CHAPTER NINE

IT WAS Sarah's turn to open the little window, but Matt had been held up over at the hospital and Jenny was asleep so it was only Lesley and Colin watching while Sarah took down the advent calendar.

'Oh, it's the fairy on top of the tree!' she said, delighted.

'Fairies—yuck!' Colin managed to look disgusted, while at the same time having a good look at the tiny picture.

'I think she's lovely,' Lesley said. 'Do you have a fairy for the tree?'

'We have a nangel instead,' Colin told her.

'He means an angel,' Sarah explained.

'That's what I said—a nangel,' Colin said, surprised.

For a moment Sarah's eyes and Lesley's eyes met, and Lesley was pleased to see that Sarah, too, was having difficulty keeping a straight face.

'We should be putting the tree up pretty soon,' Lesley said hastily. 'Another few days, maybe.' She looked at her watch. 'I think you two had better get off to bed. It could be late before Matt gets back.'

She waited until both their bedrooms were in darkness before she got out her sewing, with Murray lying on her feet. The wedding dress was almost finished for she had kept it very simple, but she wasn't too sure how she was going to manage the veil. She bunched up Sylvia's net curtain in one hand and tried it on top of the doll's head, but somehow it didn't look right.

'That was a big sigh,' Matt said, from the door. 'Bored?'

'Oh, no, just frustrated at my own lack of ability,'

Lesley replied. She put her sewing down and looked at him. 'You look tired, Matt.'

At one time she would have risen and gone into his arms in a friendly, uncomplicated, comforting way. Now—in spite of the easing between them since the journey home from Umtata—she hesitated. And because she hesitated the moment was lost.

'I can't get up,' she said a little awkwardly. 'Murray has me pinned down here.'

The dog wagged his tail at the sound of his name, but didn't move from her feet.

'He likes to do his best to make sure you stay,' Matt commented. And then said, 'Strangulated hernia. We had no choice but to do it there and then—that acute intestinal obstruction might have led to gangrene of the bowel if we'd had to wait for the helicopter to come and take him to Umtata.'

Lesley knew very well that there was considerable risk in an emergency hernia operation because of the possible danger to the bowel.

'How did it go?' she asked.

'Pretty well,' Matt said cautiously. 'We were lucky—he's in good physical shape.'

'And any danger of coughing weakening the post-operative wound?' Lesley asked.

Matt shook his head. 'No upper respiratory infection, and he isn't a smoker, fortunately. Kids in bed, I suppose?'

Lesley told him the nangel story, and she was pleased to see some of the weariness leave his lean brown face as he smiled.

'I'll get your supper,' she said. 'Patience left it ready to be heated up.'

'What did doctors do before microwaves?' Matt said when she brought the tray through five minutes later. 'Will you sit and talk to me while I eat, Lesley?'

They talked about the hospital, and about the chil-dren, and how soon the Christmas tree should be brought out and decorated, and Lesley showed Matt what she had done for the bride doll.

'I can't get the veil right, though,' she said sadly. 'I think I'll leave it for now—there's still plenty of time. More coffee?'

She stood up—and winced.

'I've been sitting over that sewing for too long,' she said. 'I think I'll have a nice long bath and go to bed.'

She could see that Matt was disappointed, but all at once she didn't feel too well and bath and bed seemed a good idea.

This time she didn't hesitate, and kissed Matt lightly.

'Don't come over,' she said. 'You should have an early night, too.'

She bent down to pat Murray, who had moved to capture Matt's feet, and winced again.

'Are you all right?' Matt asked.

'I'm fine,' Lesley assured him. 'Like I said, too long sitting over my sewing.'

But when she had had her bath and was in bed she had to admit that she really didn't feel at all well. Must be something I've eaten, she thought as she realised that, as well as the sharp pain, she did feel sick. I'm sure I'll feel better after a good night's sleep.

But a few hours later she woke to realise that she felt very much worse. She switched on the light to see the time, and caught a glimpse of her reflection in the mirror. Her face was grey, and she could feel the dampness on her forehead as the unrelenting pain gripped her.

Somehow she got out into the dark corridor and reached the door next to hers—Anna-Marie's.

'Lesley? Is something wrong?'

And then, her voice sharpening, the dark-haired girl said, 'You're ill. What is it?'

'I have this awful pain,' Lesley managed to say. 'And I feel sick.'

Gently Anna-Marie helped Lesley down onto her bed and drew a blanket over her for, although the night was warm, Lesley was shivering. Her hand on Lesley's forehead and her wrist was cool and professional.

'I'm going to get Matt,' she said quietly after a moment, and then she hurried out.

Waves of pain washed over Lesley, and she closed her eyes, wanting nothing in the world but for Matt to be there and this pain to be gone.

It seemed an eternity before she felt Matt's hand on her forehead, and then on her wrist.

'You're right, Anna-Marie, her pulse is racing and she's in shock,' he said. 'Lesley, where is the pain?'

'Abdominal—here,' Lesley told him.

'Right lower quadrant,' he murmured, and his hands were gentle as he examined her. 'Anna-Marie, get David, would you?'

Lesley looked up at him.

'Do you think it's my appendix?' she asked, knowing it was never an easy diagnosis, and he nodded.

'Looks like it,' he said. 'I'm sorry, Lesley, I can't give you anything for the pain until I get David to confirm my diagnosis.'

Lesley could feel her forehead become damp as another wave of even more acute pain washed over her. Matt's hand gripped hers hard, and she clung to it.

A moment later David Balfour hurried in with Anna-Marie, and she heard the low murmur of Matt's voice and then the younger doctor's. Then David's hands were examining her.

'What do you get?' she heard Matt ask, and even through the pain she was conscious of the tight anxiety in his voice.

'Diffuse tenderness around the umbilicus and the mid-epgastrium, and I got Roving's Sign by palpating the lower left quadrant, and she felt pain in the right lower quadrant. Extreme muscular rigidity, and right hip flexing, suggesting inflammation of the psoas muscle. Yes, appendix.'

'Just get on and do it,' Lesley managed to say.

'Let's get her to the theatre,' Matt said. 'Put her out now, David.'

Yes, please, Lesley wanted to say, then there was a small prick and the pain began to recede.

The last thing she saw was Matt's face, taut with anxiety as he and David eased her onto the stretcher.

It's an operation I've done so many times, Matt told himself as he scrubbed up.

But this time—

This time it's different because it's Lesley.

'She's out,' David said, and he checked the mask on Lesley's face.

'What do you think about the incision? McBurney or Rockey-Davis?' Matt asked.

Above the green mask David's eyes met his.

'You're the surgeon—I'm only the anaesthetist,' he said. And then, 'I'd go for the Rockey-Davis. That transverse cut is preferable if—'

If the appendix is likely to rupture.

The words didn't need to be said, Matt knew, as he took the sterilised scalpel from Anna-Marie, who was assisting, and made the first incision. He was already accustomed to having her as his theatre sister, and there was little need to give her any instructions. He was grateful for that as he worked steadily in the silence of the small theatre.

It was only when he removed the appendix that there was a palpable sigh of relief from all three of them.

'Got it in time,' Matt said, and he thought that his own voice sounded startlingly loud. 'But just in time. I'd say another half-hour and we could have been in trouble.'

He began to work on the inside stitches, glad that this was a straightforward job because he had been able to remove the diseased appendix before it ruptured.

'Keep her in Fowler's position,' he said to Anna-Marie as he finished and threw down his gloves. 'But I don't think we'll have any complications. Thanks for coming for me so quickly, Anna-Marie. And thanks for your part, David.'

Anna-Marie would, he knew, remain with Lesley until she came out of the anaesthetic. There was no need for him to stay, and he never did, after an operation was over. But this was different, and he had to force himself to walk out of the small recovery room with no more than a last quick glance at the unconscious girl in the bed.

To his surprise, it was still dark with only the first streaks of dawn in the sky.

'I think we need some coffee,' the younger doctor said, and he led the way through to the silent dining-room and switched on the electric kettle.

In all his professional life Matt had never felt like this after operating. Drained—exhausted—and foolishly anxious. Foolishly, he told himself firmly, because everything went well, and Anna-Marie is with her. And a straightforward appendectomy isn't exactly life-threatening.

'Thanks,' he said, when David handed him a mug of coffee.

'I think I'll have a couple of hours' sleep,' David said. He looked at his watch. 'Lesley should be surfacing in half an hour, Matt, if you want to go and sit with her.'

Matt opened his mouth to list all the excellent reasons why this wasn't in the least necessary. Then he closed it.

'I think I'll do that,' he said.

Anna-Marie didn't seem surprised to see him back.

'She's beginning to stir,' she said. She stood up. 'If you're going to be here for a bit I'll go and have a quick bath,' she said briskly, seeming to take his assent for granted.

Not long after she left Lesley, propped up so that she was almost sitting, moved her head restlessly.

'It's all right, Lesley, try to keep still,' Matt said, and he put his hand on her shoulders. Unexpectedly, she opened her eyes.

'Matt?' she said, bewilderment in her voice. And then, her hand gripping his, 'Don't go away, Matt. Stay with me.'

'I'll stay,' Matt promised, not quite steadily.

Her eyes closed then, and her breathing became regular and steady. Almost real sleep, instead of surfacing from an anaesthetic, Matt thought, knowing he was being less than professional about this. He tried to loosen his hand, but Lesley's hand tightened on his. After a while he felt his eyelids droop, and he put his head down on the bed.

He'd had no intention of falling asleep but slowly, through mists, he heard his name.

'Matt? Matt?'

Lesley's eyes had lost their unfocussed look now.

'What are you doing here?' she asked him.

'You asked me to stay,' he told her. Relief and amusement bubbled up inside him because she sounded quite aggressive, and she looked very young with her hair tousled. 'You said, "Don't go away. Stay with me." And, besides, you wouldn't let me go.'

'Oh,' Lesley said faintly.

A wave of colour flooded her cheeks as she looked at her hand, still gripping his tightly.

'Tell me about my appendix,' she said surprisingly firmly, and he told her how the operation had gone. Just as he finished Anna-Marie came back wearing a clean uniform, her dark hair still damp.

'You look more human now, Lesley,' she said. 'Nurse Thorpe was on duty last night so she knows you're coming into General, but I thought I'd get back early to organise things on the ward.'

'You'd better go home now, Matt,' Lesley said. 'You need to shower and have breakfast and—and see the children.'

He could see that she was still embarrassed about what she had said, although the colour had faded from her cheeks now. But he could see the shadows under her grey eyes.

'All right, Boss Lady, I'll go,' he said. 'And you need to rest. I'll see you later.'

'You don't—' she began.

'Oh, but I do,' he returned. 'You're my patient, after all. Isn't she, Sister Botha?'

'Of course, Dr Turner,' Anna-Marie agreed. She looked down at Lesley and, to Matt's surprise, she smiled. 'And you are my patient, too, so you will have to do what I tell you!'

Lesley managed a smile.

'After the way I felt last night, I think I'd do what anyone told me,' she admitted.

'I'll remember that,' Matt said, his voice low. 'See you later, Sister Grant.'

Anna-Marie Botha had turned away.

'Anything you say, Doctor, dear,' Lesley returned cheekily.

Matt walked back across the compound, opened the gate and walked along the garden path. It was just beginning to be light now and, to his surprise, he realised he was whistling. He stopped, but not quickly enough for as he opened the front door Sarah appeared, rubbing her eyes, Murray beside her.

'Are you just home now, Uncle Matt?' she asked sleepily. 'That must have been a long operation. I'm glad Lesley said we shouldn't wait up for you.'

Matt hesitated, but only for a moment. The children would have to know soon enough.

'I had another emergency operation, Sarah,' he said quietly. 'In the middle of the night. Lesley had to have her appendix taken out.'

All the colour left the little girl's face.

'Is Lesley—is Lesley going to be all right?' she said shakily.

Matt knelt down and put his arms around her.

'Lesley is going to be fine,' he assured her. 'She'll

have to stay in hospital for a day or two, but I'll take her stitches out in five days and she'll be able to go back to work soon after that. Tell you what, I'll have a quick shower and you and I can have breakfast together before Colin and Jenny wake. And later today I'll take the three of you over to see Lesley. How's that?'

Sarah smiled, a smile that lit up her whole face.

'That's fine, Uncle Matt,' she said sedately. 'I'll go and dress.'

When she had gone Matt sat down on the swing seat, Murray at his feet. She asked me to stay, he thought. She wanted me to be with her.

'Damn it,' he said aloud, startling the dog. 'I am not giving up.' Murray wagged his tail.

'I love her,' Matt told him. 'And I think maybe— just maybe—she is beginning to realise that she loves me, too.'

Maybe.

Again, maybe not.

Soberly, he reminded himself that there was really nothing he could or should make out of what Lesley had said. All right, she had asked him to stay but she hadn't even been conscious. And gripping his hand the way she had—that, too, had been an unconscious gesture, a meaningless one. She was just as likely to have held onto Anna-Marie or David if they had been there at that moment.

'Uncle Matt?' Sarah said from the doorway. She had pulled on a cotton dress and sandals and, with her thick brown hair drawn back in a velvet band, she looked so like her mother that there was a catch in Matt's throat.

'I'll be with you in five minutes, Sarah,' he said. 'Patience isn't in yet—can you organise something for the two of us?'

Sarah nodded.

'Muesli and toast and coffee?' she asked him.

'Great,' Matt replied.

And, in spite of his gloomy thoughts about Lesley,

he couldn't help feeling his heart lifting as his niece smiled at him.

It was a very strange thing, Lesley found, being a patient instead of being a nurse. She hadn't been a patient since she had her tonsils out at the age of five.

Anna-Marie was an efficient and extremely professional nurse but, more than that, Lesley realised very soon that she had that inbuilt ability to inspire confidence in her patients which not every nurse had. Lesley found herself meekly doing what she was told, and feeling better and more comfortable for the dark-haired sister's care.

'Thank you for reacting as quickly as you did, Anna-Marie,' she said later, when she had been moved to a bed in the general ward.

'I'm glad you came to me,' Anna-Marie said, and Lesley didn't like to say that she had been in such pain that she had only just managed to reach the nearest door.

It was a strange thing, though, she began to realise. Somehow, by going to Anna-Marie for help she had changed something in their relationship. The coolness and the hostility had gone.

She slept a fair bit through that day, vaguely conscious of the work of the general ward going on around her—vaguely interested, but finding that her eyelids would close and she would drift off again to sleep.

'Dr Turner was here on his ward round but you were asleep,' Anna-Marie told her briskly around lunchtime. 'He said he'd be back later when he finished in Casualty. Do you want anything to eat?'

Lesley shook her head.

'I'd love a cup of tea, though,' she said, and a few minutes later Anna-Marie helped her to drink some tea.

It was the tea, Lesley thought, that helped her to throw off the last mists of the anaesthetic.

'How on earth are we going to manage in Maternity?' she said, dismayed, when Matt came in later.

'We'll just have to,' Matt replied. 'Peggy Thorpe has a friend who does agency nursing, and she's trying to get in touch with her. Fortunately, you don't have many babies due in the next couple of weeks.'

He smiled, but his eyes were concerned.

'You don't look too great yet,' he said, 'But the children want to see you. Can you cope, just for a quick visit?'

He hesitated.

'Sarah was pretty worried when I told her,' he said. 'I'm not too sure if she'll relax until she sees you for herself.'

In fact, Jenny was the only one unaffected by seeing Lesley in bed, she realised when Matt brought them in. Colin's freckles stood out against a rather white little face and Sarah's brown eyes were anxious.

'We brought you flowers,' Colin said, and he handed her a small bunch of flowers from the garden. Lesley sniffed them, the mixed scent of the frangipani and the magnolia fragrant after the smells of the ward.

'And Sarah drawed you a card,' Colin told her.

Lesley took the card, with its careful writing and a drawing of a heart.

'Get Well Soon,' the card said. 'We Love You, Lesley.'

She opened it, and there was a drawing of what she realised must be Murray, wagging his tail. And Sarah's name, and Colin's, and a big J from Jenny.

'It's lovely,' she said, not quite steadily. 'The flowers and the card—thank you all so much. I can't hug you, but please give me a kiss.'

Sarah kissed her, and then Colin did, and then Matt lifted Jenny up. The little girl's cheek was soft, and her baby hands were warm around Lesley's neck.

And above her fair curly head Lesley found Matt's dark eyes resting on her face.

Resting, and waiting.

*   *   *

'Quite a responsibility Matt has taken on,' Anna-Marie commented as Matt and the children left, Colin turning at the door of the ward to wave, Jenny giving her sunny smile to all the other patients and Sarah with a last anxious look at Lesley.

'Yes, it is,' Lesley agreed. She hesitated, but only for a moment. 'It was a promise he made to his brother.'

The dark-haired sister's hands were efficient but gentle as she moved Lesley's pillows and made her more comfortable.

'I did hear that—from Sylvia. But still a big thing to take on—three children, and coming to the hospital here.' Her dark eyes met Lesley's. 'We were all surprised when we heard that Matt was coming here, instead of taking the children to England.'

'So was I,' Lesley admitted, and she remembered how she had felt when Matt had told her.

'Matt is different from Peter,' Anna-Marie said thoughtfully. 'Peter was—more serious, perhaps more dedicated. When Matt came I thought he was the wrong kind of doctor, the wrong kind of man, for this hospital. But he has changed. Or don't you see that?'

'Oh, yes, he's changed,' Lesley agreed wholeheartedly. And then, surprising herself, she said slowly, 'Sometimes he seems like a different person from the Matt I knew in London. Like a stranger.'

Anna-Marie straightened up.

'But you've changed, too, Lesley,' she said.

The nurse-aide came over then, and the Afrikaans sister went with her to the other side of the ward to the screened bed where Matt's emergency hernia patient was.

And Lesley, watching, thought with amazement, Here I am on the point of having a heart-to-heart with Anna-Marie Botha! Who would have thought it?

As she lay in bed watching the dark-haired sister as she worked—changing dressings, not only supervising but helping to wash patients, giving out food, dealing

with medication, answering relatives' questions—
Lesley was very glad that the hostility Anna-Marie had
felt for her seemed to have gone.

She said I've changed, too, Lesley thought. And I
suppose that's true. And she's seen me change, and
maybe she thought she'd been a bit quick in judging me.

But the real breakthrough had clearly been when
she'd gone to Anna-Marie for help, she knew that. And
now she was even more glad that that was where she
had turned, whether consciously or not.

Sylvia and Ken came for a brief visit in the afternoon
and Lesley, answering their questions, agreed with them
that, yes, it was very strange to be a patient instead of
a nurse, and thought that perhaps Sylvia did look as if
the new treatment was doing something positive for
her. Even if it was no more than to keep her in remission
for longer.

Ken went to talk to one of the other patients, and
Lesley asked Sylvia how she was.

'I really think I feel a little better,' the older woman
said quietly. 'This new treatment doesn't seem to make
me feel nauseous, and that alone is a help. I go to
Umtata for a check-up next week so we'll see if Dr Lund
agrees with me. And if he's prepared to recommend that
I stay on the treatment.'

That night, when Peggy Thorpe arrived for night
duty, Anna-Marie came to ask Lesley if there was anything she wanted from her room.

'I don't think so,' Lesley said. 'You brought all the
toilet things I need and a clean nightie. Oh—there is
one thing. On the third shelf of my wardrobe you'll
find the sewing I'm doing. If you could bring it to me
I might be able to do some. Don't bring the doll, though,
in case Sarah comes to visit.'

She told Anna-Marie about Sarah's request for a
bride doll.

'I'll bring your sewing, but not tonight,' Anna-Marie
said firmly. 'By tomorrow you can perhaps do some—

tonight you must rest. How do your stitches feel?'

Lesley moved cautiously.

'Not bad,' she admitted, with some surprise. 'Tender, but nothing seems to be pulling.'

'Dr Turner has prescribed more of the painkillers for you,' Anna-Marie said. 'Let Nurse Thorpe know if you need any during the night.'

There were no official visiting hours in the small hospital because the visiting relatives often had to come so far that they were allowed to visit at almost any time. But because of that there were seldom any visitors in the evening, and the ward was quiet and the lights dimmed early. Lesley, still drowsy from the anaesthetic, fell asleep sooner than she thought she would, waking from time to time to see Peggy Thorpe's stout little figure moving swiftly but softly around the ward. There was something very reassuring and comforting about that.

She wasn't sure how late it was when she woke to see Matt at the other side of the room with Peggy Thorpe. With his hernia patient, Lesley realised, and a little later, when Matt came over to her bed, he told her that he had been checking for oedema at the wound site.

'But he's fine,' he said. 'No problems. And how about you?'

'No problems with me either,' Lesley told him. 'That was two emergencies in one night, Matt—good going.'

'I could do with easier nights,' Matt admitted. 'If you do anything like this again you might choose a better time.'

'I'll try,' Lesley promised. 'How are the children?'

'They're fine,' he said. 'They're going to bring you the advent calendar tomorrow to show you the robin wearing a scarf from today, and to open tomorrow's picture. Colin thinks they should bring Murray to visit you, but I said no, thanks.'

'And Sarah?' Lesley asked.

'I think she's all right now,' Matt said slowly. 'She

did keep asking me if you really were all right. I think the way you looked today worried her.'

'How did I look?' Lesley asked him.

He smiled.

'Not very great,' he told her. 'My Scottish grand-mother had a lovely word for the way you looked—peely-wallie. Hey, don't laugh, your stitches will hurt and you'll wake the other patients!'

'I don't know what it means, but it sounds pretty bad,' Lesley said. 'I feel a lot better now, though. I must have slept for most of the day.'

'You look better,' Matt assured her. He stood up and looked down at her with his dark head on one side. 'Far from being yourself, but—yes, better.'

He smiled.

'Much as I would like to, I can't kiss you goodnight,' he said softly. 'Preferential treatment—I'd have to go round them all if I did that. Can you take a rain check on it?'

'I'll do that,' Lesley agreed, smiling, too, and she watched his tall figure stride down the ward to have a word with Peggy Thorpe, sitting at a table with a small lamp on it, before he left.

Somewhere inside her there was a warm little glow. Just a little visit, some friendly exchanges, something to laugh at. Something, she thought wonderingly, that seemed to bridge the gap between the old Matt and this new Matt.

She remembered now that moment when she had surfaced from the anaesthetic and seen Matt's dark rumpled head on the bed beside her. She couldn't remember asking him to stay with her, but she did remember the feel of his hand as she held onto it. So, consciously or not, she thought, I wanted him there beside me.

But—

And always she came back to that but. A big but. Two big buts, if she was honest. But—how real, and how valid, were her feelings for this new Matt? She couldn't discount that bewildering physical magnetism which was so different from any feelings she had had for Matt before, but a long-term commitment had to be based on something more than that. And the other but. But—what about the children? The children she had become so fond of, but the children who were from now on part and parcel of Matt's life.

There were, she knew very well, these questions and more to be answered—important things to be thought through. Matt's eyes last night, meeting hers above Jenny's fair curls—asking questions, waiting.

But I can't do anything about any of that now, she thought with some relief as she felt herself drifting off to sleep again.

The next morning Anna-Marie brought Lesley's sewing to her and agreed that, propped up as she was, a little sewing wouldn't do any harm.

Lesley sewed the hem of the bride's dress and finished off the sleeves, then had another look at the net for the veil.

'I can't think what to do with the veil,' she told Anna-Marie later. 'Maybe I'll just have to gather it and sew it onto the doll's hair, but Sarah will want to take it off.'

Anna-Marie took the piece of net curtain in her hands, and looked at it.

'I might be able to do something,' she said. 'Can I try?'

'I'd be only too pleased to have help with it,' Lesley assured her. 'I do so want it to be nice for Sarah.'

The Afrikaans girl's dark eyes rested on Lesley.

'They're important to you, the children,' she said, and it wasn't a question.

'Yes, they are,' Lesley replied slowly. And for a moment she had a strange thought—too important? Am I letting them become too important to me, and me to them, if—if I'm going to walk out of their lives when Christmas is over?

It was a disturbing thought, and she knew that it was a thought she would have to face up to—to deal with in a way that was completely honest—before long.

An hour after Anna-Marie went off duty and handed over to the night staff she came back into the ward with a large bag in her hand.

'I didn't want to risk Sarah being here,' she said breathlessly. 'But what do you think, Lesley?'

She lifted the flaxen-haired doll from the bag, and Lesley gasped. The doll was dressed in the dress she had made, but the wide satin sash tied around it made it perfect. And on her head there was a circlet of tiny pearls, with the net of the veil carefully sewn onto it so that it fell in misty folds over the doll's face.

'Anna-Marie, she's perfect,' Lesley said. 'Sarah will love her.'

The sister flushed with pleasure.

'I thought of that bracelet I had,' she said. 'It makes a little tiara for her.' And then, anxiously, she said, 'Do you mind me doing it? I've always enjoyed sewing, and I sometimes dress dolls for my brother's little girls.'

'Mind?' Lesley replied. 'Anna-Marie, I'm so grateful. I did want to do some of her clothes but I really was struggling with the veil.'

Anna-Marie smiled, and Lesley thought how pretty she was with her face softened like that and her dark hair unpinned.

'I think I'll do bride dolls for Karen's and Magda's birthdays. I enjoyed this little bit so much.'

She stood up.

'I'll take her back to your room and hide her again— I haven't had supper yet, but I wanted to finish her and let you see her.'

It was, once again, a quiet evening, and Matt didn't come to the ward. Peggy Thorpe told Lesley that Agnes

Cekiso had had to call him to help with a difficult delivery.

'I'm on tomorrow night,' she said cheerfully. 'I'm glad it happened tonight.'

Turning away with the medication tray in her hands, she thought of something.

'You'll be glad to know my friend, Helen—the one who's doing agency nursing—is coming in a couple of days. She's a midwife, too, so between the two of us and Agnes we should manage until you're back.'

The next day Lesley caught Matt when he came in to see a young boy who had been brought to the hospital with a badly burned leg.

'When can I get out?' Lesley demanded. 'They're always short of beds in General.'

'Yes, I've been thinking about that,' Matt said. He ran his hand through his thick dark hair. 'This is the third day after the op. There's no infection, the wound is healing nicely and you're right here on the spot. I'll take the stitches out in another three days, probably. You could go out tomorrow, I think, but—'

He lifted her chart from the end of the bed and studied it.

'Look, I'm going to change that kid's dressing now. The analgesic will have taken effect and he'll be reasonably comfortable. I'll have a word with Anna-Marie about you going out tomorrow.'

It wasn't a large ward, and from her bed Lesley watched as Matt, with Anna-Marie assisting him, gently removed the soiled dressing. She wasn't close enough to see the cleansing and debridement, but she saw Anna-Marie hand Matt the impregnated fine gauze and then the tubular mesh overdressing. The burn was on the boy's shin, and when the dressing had been completed the bandaged leg was propped up on a pillow. To prevent oedema, Lesley knew.

Matt straightened and touched the boy's thin shoulder, and said something to him. Lesley, watching, saw a smile crease the young face as he replied to Matt.

He always was a good doctor, she knew that, but seeing him here, in the mission hospital, she realised that there was a new dimension now in Matt the doctor—a dimension of caring, of involvement, that she didn't think had been there before.

She was thinking about this when Matt stopped beside her bed again.

'Anna-Marie will change your dressing in the morning,' he said. 'And you can get out in the afternoon.'

'And when——?' Lesley began, impatiently.

'When can you go back to work? Ten days' recuperation,' he said, and the firmness of his voice told her that there would be no discussion of this.

Dismayed, she counted up.

'But that means three days after Christmas!' she said. 'Matt, there are all sorts of things we need to be doing for Christmas for the children. Surely it's time for the tree now?'

'I did tell you you might have chosen a better time,' Matt said mildly. 'Lesley, we've talked about the tree, the children and I, and they won't consider it without you. Maybe in a couple of nights we'll do it—you could lie on the couch and direct operations.'

Lesley thought about that.

'I suppose I could,' she agreed. 'I'm—not as much use as I should be, though.'

Suddenly, to her horror, she felt tears fill her eyes. She turned her head, but not quickly enough.

'Hey,' Matt said, and the gentleness of his voice unnerved her even more than his hand on hers. 'Tears, Lesley?'

He took out his handkerchief and dried her eyes, awkwardly but gently.

'The anaesthetic does that sometimes to people,' he said comfortingly. 'Makes them weepy, I mean.'

'Sorry, Matt,' Lesley said, and she took the handkerchief from him and scrubbed her eyes.

'I was thinking, though,' Matt said, 'it might be a good idea if you were to come and stay in the house. Patience can keep an eye on you, and the children would love having you there.' He hesitated, and then said, his voice level, 'And so would I. I don't like the thought of you in the nurses' home—it's pretty bleak.'

It was a tempting thought but Lesley, after a moment, shook her head.

'No, Matt,' she said regretfully.

'Why not?' he asked, and there was a rather aggressive tilt to his chin which was so like Colin could sometimes look that the last of the tears were gone and Lesley had to smile.

'It would put us all in a—in a false position,' she said.

She didn't want to go into it any further, but he knew what she was saying.

'What I could do,' she said, thinking about it, 'is stay in my own room, but come over for most of the day. How about that?'

After a moment Matt nodded.

'It will do,' he said. And then, 'I'd feel happier with you under my closer supervision, but you won't do anything foolish, will you?'

'Not with Anna-Marie in the next room,' Lesley assured him.

She would be glad to be out of hospital, but she had to admit that it had been a salutary experience, being a patient. She could understand now how it felt to be confined to bed, dependent on other people for your every need. She hoped that she had always been an understanding and a sympathetic nurse, but she was certain that this experience would make her more so.

The next morning, when Anna-Marie had changed the dressing on her wound and had expressed satisfaction that it was healing nicely, Lesley said something of this to her.

'I know what you mean,' Anna-Marie agreed. 'When I was in my final year I was in a car crash, and I had a fractured pelvis. Those weeks of lying immobile taught me things I could never have learned in any other way.'

'I'm glad my experience is only a short one,' Lesley said feelingly.

She had already been up, walking around the ward, but somehow it felt different to be dressed and walking along the corridor.

'I feel as if I'm walking like an old woman,' she said when they reached the door of her room.

'It will be easier when you get your stitches out,' Anna-Marie told her. 'Now, you're to lie down until about four—I'll have someone bring you something to eat—and then you can walk very gently across the compound to the doctor's house. And you mustn't be too late coming back.'

'I'll behave,' Lesley promised. She smiled, and Anna-Marie smiled back.

Later, as she walked slowly across the compound in the heat of the afternoon, she saw the three children and Murray waiting at the gate for her.

'Hurry up, Lesley,' Colin called.

'Be careful,' Sarah said, at the same time.

Jenny, joyously, called, 'Lesley come!' and held out her small golden arms.

They led her to a couch on the stoep, and told her that Uncle Matt had carried it out this morning.

'Because you won't be comfortable on the swing seat,' Sarah said earnestly. She arranged the cushions behind Lesley, and asked if she was all right like that.

'Miss Lesley, you are to do nothing,' Patience said severely a little later, when she came out carrying a tray with tea, orange juice and biscuits on it. 'I will pour, and Sarah will bring your cup to you.'

She looked at Colin and Jenny, sitting on the floor beside Lesley's couch, with Murray right beside them.

'Why you have to sit right beside Miss Lesley?' she asked them.

''Cos we like her,' Colin answered. 'Don't we, Jenny?'

'Like her,' Jenny echoed, and she moved even closer.

'I don't mind, Patience,' Lesley said, meaning it. 'Sarah, come and sit here, too.'

A great deal seemed to have happened in the time she'd been in hospital, and Colin and Sarah were eager to tell her everything.

'We got presents from our gran and grandpa,' Colin said. 'They came with the hospital things from Umtata today. And last night Gran phoned.'

'I was to tell Lesley that,' Sarah said reproachfully, and Colin had the grace to look guilty and to mumble that he forgot.

'Gran phoned, and she said she wished she could be here with us for Christmas, but Grandpa isn't very well and, besides, the heat here doesn't really agree with them,' Sarah said.

''Cos they're old,' Colin explained.

'But Gran says she's so glad Uncle Matt and you are here,' Sarah went on, ignoring the interruption. She looked meaningly at Colin. 'And she said we aren't to open our presents until Christmas Day.'

'Me now,' Colin said. 'Lesley, we're practising to do a Christmas play. Sylvia does one with us every year. It's called—what is it called, Sarah?'

'It's a Nativity play,' Sarah said. 'And the day after tomorrow is when we do it.'

'And we're all coming to see it—everyone who can be moved—from the hospital,' Matt said from the steps.

'Uncle Matt, we didn't hear you,' Colin said, running to him.

'I'm not surprised,' Matt said. 'You were all too busy speaking.'

He came over to the couch and sat on the edge of it.

'How are you doing, Lesley?' he asked.

'Fine,' Lesley assured him. 'Just fine.'

'Tonight,' he told her, 'I'm taking you back right after supper. But tomorrow night. . .'

He paused, and looked at the children.

'Shall we tell her?' he said, and all three of them chorused yes, Murray joining in with a loud bark.

'Tomorrow night we're going to put up the tree,' Matt said. 'We've got all the decorations ready.'

It was when they had almost finished eating, and Matt and Lesley were having coffee, that Lesley realised that Sarah was very quiet. When the little girl slipped quietly out of the room Lesley followed her along to her room.

As she had half expected, Sarah was sitting on her bed with her head bent.

'What is it, Sarah?' Lesley asked gently from the door.

Sarah shook her head mutely. Lesley sat down beside her, and took the small hands in hers.

'Are you thinking about last Christmas?' she asked. Sarah nodded.

'I was remembering how we did the tree last year,' she said shakily. 'Jenny was so small, but when she saw it she clapped her hands and she laughed. Mummy was holding her, and Daddy took that lovely picture.'

She pointed to the photo frame beside her bed. Clare, with Jenny in her arms—both of them laughing. Sarah's brown eyes were very bright, and she was biting her lip.

'It's all right to cry, Sarah,' Lesley said. 'Sometimes it helps to cry.'

'I shouldn't cry,' Sarah told her. 'I'm the big one— I shouldn't cry.'

Lesley put her arms around the small shoulders.

'You're not so big, pet,' she said. 'Not too big to cry.'

The tears came then, and Lesley held Sarah in her arms.

CHAPTER TEN

WHEN the tears were over Lesley dried Sarah's eyes.

'You're never too big to cry, Sarah,' she said steadily. 'And it's better to let yourself cry than to keep the tears shut inside.'

Sarah's eyes—even swollen with tears—were clearer, less shadowed.

'I had this sort of lump here sometimes,' she said, and she touched her throat. 'And you know, Lesley, it isn't there now.' She thought for a moment. 'Maybe it will come back when I feel sad again.'

'I'm sure it will,' Lesley replied. 'And you will feel sad again, Sarah, because it's such a sad thing, losing your mummy and your daddy. But let yourself cry when you need to.'

She brushed the little girl's hair back from her forehead.

'Your mummy and daddy would understand that you feel sad, but I think, Sarah, that they would want you to find things to be happy about—things to take away some of the sadness.'

She held out her hand.

'Can we go back to the others now?' she asked, and Sarah nodded.

But as they left her room she said, 'Sometimes I think it's easier for Colin and Jenny, 'cos they don't remember so much. Colin does, sometimes, then he forgets again.'

Matt didn't say anything when they went back out to the stoep but later, when he took her back across to the nurses' home—leaving the children with Patience to get ready for bed because he refused to let Lesley stay up any longer—she told him about Sarah's tears.

'I do think she felt better for letting herself cry,' she said. 'Poor little girl, she does feel her responsibilities so much, Matt.'

'I know,' Matt agreed. 'I'm always so pleased when I see her laugh, or even argue with Colin, or just be a normal nine-year-old.'

'So am I,' Lesley said. 'But you know, Matt, I think that's happening more and more. She'll always be more quiet, more serious, than Colin, and than Jenny, but— yes, we need to help her to be a normal nine-year-old.'

She had said 'we' unthinkingly. Matt made no comment, but she could see that he hadn't missed it and she felt warm colour in her cheeks.

'You'd better get back to them,' she said hastily, and his dark eyes were, after a moment's questioning, amused as he agreed.

'And you're to get right off to bed,' he told her. 'You've had a long enough day.'

He kissed her, lightly, undemandingly, his hands on her shoulders. For one unguarded, instinctive moment Lesley moved closer to him, and she felt his immediate response.

'Hey,' he said, 'that isn't fair. Any more and I'll be forgetting your stitches. Goodnight, Lesley.'

'Goodnight, Matt,' she said, more than a little shaken by the way she had felt. Before she closed the door she watched his tall figure stride across the compound back to the house.

He was right. It had been a long day, she thought, and, interesting as it had been being a patient, she was very glad to be back in her little room again—brightened now with the rugs and the curtains Sylvia had organised for her.

And I will be even more glad, she thought, easing herself into bed, to get these stitches out. Not because of what Matt had said, she told herself hastily, just to be a stage further on.

She spent the next day quietly, sometimes lying on

the couch at the house and sometimes getting up to walk around the garden with Murray padding along beside her. The children were with Sylvia until almost four, practising for their Nativity play.

'Have you been lonely without us?' Colin asked her when they came back, and Lesley assured him truthfully that she had.

'How is the play going?' she asked.

'Fine,' he said casually. 'You know, Lesley, last year I was a sheep, and this year I'm one of the shepherds. That's much more important, isn't it?'

'It's quite a promotion,' Lesley agreed. 'What are you, Sarah?'

'I'm Mary,' Sarah told her. 'And Jenny is a baby angel. We have a doll for Baby Jesus—it's safer than a real baby. We did have a real baby once but it cried too much so Sylvia said a doll would be safer.'

'I'm sure it is,' Lesley said. 'I'm so much looking forward to the play.'

She had never seen supper eaten so quickly, or three children help to clear the table so efficiently and get themselves bathed and ready for bed, for Matt had decided this had to be done before the tree. Matt carried the couch inside, set it near the brick fireplace and placed pillows to prop Lesley up. From a large cardboard box he and Colin drew the tree out.

'It always looks flat now, but when we straighten out all the branches it looks quite real,' Sarah said.

And it did. Set on its stand, in front of the empty fireplace, it looked a very respectable Christmas tree.

'Now we do the ormanets,' Colin told her.

'Ornaments,' Sarah corrected him.

'I said that,' he returned, and glared at his sister.

'How do we go about this?' Matt asked, intervening.

'We set them all out on the coffee-table,' Sarah told him, 'and the low ones we can put on the tree ourselves, but the high ones we—' She hesitated, then went on steadily, 'We hand them to you, and you put them on.'

'What can I do?' Lesley asked, and Sarah handed her a plastic bag with some small cardboard boxes inside it.

'You can open them up,' she said. 'They're the precious ones, the ones that break.'

Carefully Lesley took out a tiny crystal Nativity scene, then three tinkling bells and half a dozen shining glass balls. She handed them, one by one, to Sarah, and watched as the little girl carefully hung them on the tree.

'Now I do the wooden ones,' Colin said, and he took out a small wooden rocking horse, bright scarlet elves and silver-painted pine cones. Jenny was allowed to place some of these, and then Matt draped the lights over the tree, followed by some tinsel.

'Now the pretend snow,' Colin said, and the three children put pieces of cotton wool on the green branches.

'And now we do the angel,' Sarah said when the tree was brightly and gaily decorated.

Carefully, gently, she handed Matt a small angel, her halo and her wings tipped with gold and her eyes closed in an angelic way, Lesley thought.

'She's beautiful,' she said.

'One of the nurses sent her to us. She lives in Germany, and when she went back there she sent us our angel,' Sarah said.

'You get boy angels and you get girl angels,' Colin explained. 'The Angel Gabriel is a boy angel, but you do get girls as well. You even get baby angels, like Jenny is going to be in the play.'

For a moment Lesley's eyes met Matt's, as they both agreed that of course you did.

'Bed now for all of you—you, too, Lesley,' Matt said firmly.

'We don't mind, acksherly, 'cos going to bed and sleeping brings Christmas more quickly,' Colin said. 'And when it's Christmas Eve, and we hang up our stockings, we go to sleep so quickly 'cos Father Christmas doesn't like children to see him.'

Stockings, Lesley thought, dismayed. We didn't think about stockings!

'Where do you hang your stockings?' she asked carefully, seeing her own dismay mirrored in Matt's eyes.

'We hang them up on the end of our beds,' Colin said. 'And Father Christmas sees by the light of the candles.'

'Candles?' Matt asked.

'When we go to sleep on Christmas Eve,' Sarah explained, 'we each have a little candle beside our beds, and it burns until it burns away.'

'Last year my candle was a reindeer,' Colin told them. And then, regretfully, 'But in the morning he was all melted away.'

'And melt away is what you have to do now,' Matt said, and this had Colin rolling on the floor with mirth, declaring that he was melting away now.

Jenny was almost asleep, and Matt carried her through to her room. Lesley followed to say goodnight to the children, knowing she would be glad to reach her own bed but knowing, too, that there were things she and Matt had to talk about.

'Stockings and candles,' Matt said when they went back through. 'What are we going to do about that?'

Without needing to be told, Lesley lay down on the couch.

'Ken and Sylvia are going to Umtata the day after tomorrow,' she said. 'It's a bit of a cheek, when Sylvia has her check-up and Ken has the hospital and the mission supplies to organise, but we do need help. Sylvia will be busy with the play tomorrow, but I could try to have a quick word with her. I don't think she'd mind.'

'I don't mind at all,' Sylvia assured her the next morning. She smiled. 'It will give me something to think about on the journey and if I'm kept waiting at the hospital. Candles, now. I don't think we'd find anything but ordinary white candles in Umtata, but Julie was into candles last year and she had moulds. We couldn't manage reindeer, but there might be something. I'll look out the moulds for you. Oh, it was Anna-Marie who helped Julie—she'd give you a hand.'

'And things for stockings?' Lesley asked. 'Just little plastic toys—anything cheap and cheerful. If we give you some money just get whatever you can. Are you sure you'll have time?'

'We'll manage,' Sylvia assured her. 'We used to do the same for our two so I'm not inexperienced. Lesley, I'll have to go. I have to have our last rehearsal. See you tonight.'

The general ward was where the Nativity play was to take place, and in the afternoon Lesley went over to see if she could help.

'Certainly not,' Anna-Marie told her firmly. 'You haven't even got your stitches out yet. Fortunately, we haven't anyone seriously ill or who's just been operated on at the moment. We'll move the beds close together at the far end, and we'll bring in some chairs from the hall at the mission for the patients who can sit and for the rest of the audience. Off you go and have a rest now.'

The general ward looked quite different that evening for, as well as the beds being re-arranged and the rows of chairs, there were Christmas decorations, paper streamers and brightly coloured bells. From the door at the far end Lesley could hear children's voices— Colin's sometimes rising above the rest. She managed to keep a seat for Matt, and just in time he slipped in and sat beside her.

'Gashed arm had to be stitched,' he told her briefly, and he pointed to an old man at the end of the row of seats. 'The old fellow there.'

The old man, seeing Matt looking at him, smiled a wide, toothless smile and waved his unbandaged arm.

'I don't think he minds at all, now that he's landed for this,' Matt said.

The blankets hiding the stage were drawn apart then, and the buzz of talking in the audience stopped as they looked at the three shepherds. From somewhere unseen, Sylvia's voice, clear and low, began to tell the Christmas story. The three small shepherds wore large and loose T-shirts with striped towels on their heads.

'Is that your dressing-gown cord round Colin's head?' Lesley whispered, and Matt nodded.

Sylvia's voice was silent then, and the shepherds, with unseen back-up, sang *While shepherds watched their flocks at night.*

After this the angels appeared. Jenny, the smallest one, had her hand held firmly by the biggest angel. And all, without exception, looked really angelic, Lesley thought.

When the angels had gone the shepherds held a conference.

'Yes, let's follow the star.'

'But what about our sheep?'

When they had decided to follow the star, taking their sheep with them, Colin's voice came above the others, 'Hey, Sam, that's my sheep!'

He pushed the small shepherd next to him, and took the toy sheep Sam had lifted up. Glaring fiercely, he marched off-stage, accompanied by a ripple of amusement from the audience and a loudly whispered 'Colin!' from an out-of-sight Sylvia.

The wise men appeared next, and Lesley recognised the small son of one of her patients. *We three kings of orient are*, had the unseen back-up again, and now some of the audience joined in.

Then, after a small flurry and a blanket held up, the manger was seen. Sarah, with a blue cloak, made a sweet and tender Mary, and Patience's nephew a tall, stalwart Joseph.

Lesley, looking at Sarah's smooth brown head bent over the Baby Jesus in his crib, felt her eyes prick with tears as the children sang *Away in a Manger.* Last year

Peter and Clare had been here to see their children take part in the nativity play. Now—

Matt's hand covered hers, and after a moment she returned the warm comforting pressure and managed to smile.

Silent Night was the final carol, and then Sylvia led the children out to bow to the audience.

'And I doubt if any West End play had a warmer reception than this one,' Lesley said, as she and Matt rose to help to hand out cups of tea and plates of sandwiches and cakes.

'You're not to be on your feet too long,' Matt told her, and she promised that soon she would sit down.

'We were jolly good, weren't we?' Colin said when the shepherds and the angels and the wise men, and Mary and Joseph, still in their costumes but each holding a small tin of Coke and a large sticky bun, joined the audience.

'You were very good,' Matt agreed. 'Sarah, you made a lovely Mary.' He lifted the smallest angel up. 'Jenny, you were a perfect angel.'

Five minutes later the smallest angel, almost asleep, was carried away in Patience's arms to be put to bed. The rest of the cast was fading, too, Lesley could see, and she could see also that Anna-Marie and Peggy Thorpe were doing their best to begin to get their ward back to normal and their patients reminded of the hospital routine.

Colin was sitting down on a bale of hay beside the manger with the other shepherds, all three of them looking very sleepy. Sarah's eyes were drooping as she helped Sylvia to move the crib out of the ward.

'I think we should get the children home,' Lesley murmured.

'Good idea,' Matt agreed. He looked around. 'Look, you go ahead with Sarah. I'll give a hand to move some of the beds and the chairs, and then I'll carry Colin over—he's almost asleep.'

There was something very pleasant about the feel of Sarah's hand in hers, Lesley thought as they walked across from the hospital to the house.

'You know what?' she said as she helped Sarah to put her cotton nightie on. 'For the first time tonight I really did feel like it was Christmas. I suppose it's because the weather is so different from the Christmases I've known. Even the tree didn't make me feel like this. But now—yes, I do believe it's almost Christmas.'

'Daddy used to feel like that,' Sarah said, and there was no unsteadiness in her voice. 'Mummy didn't because she lived in Cape Town, and she was used to warm Christmases, but Daddy said it took him quite a few years before he got used to Christmas when it's hot.'

She got into bed, and Lesley kissed her.

'You should go to bed, too, Lesley,' Sarah said sleepily. 'I'm so glad you were there tonight, and I'm not so worried about Christmas now, with. . .'

Her voice trailed off, and the dark lashes lay on her cheeks.

And I'm glad, too, that I was there tonight, Lesley thought, and that I'll be here for Christmas. She stood up, and looked down at the sleeping child. As she turned away she heard the front door open and close. Matt, with Colin.

Murray, who had settled on the rug beside Sarah's bed, changed his mind and went off, ears alert and tail wagging, to Colin's room next door. Lesley followed him, putting Sarah's light off.

Matt had just put Colin down on the bed, and he hadn't heard her at the door. As Lesley stood there she saw Colin stir and murmur something.

'It's all right, Colin, I'm here,' Matt said softly, and the dark head on the pillow was still.

As Lesley watched Matt eased the little boy's shepherd costume off him and put his Mickey Mouse pyjamas on him. His big brown hands were a little awkward, but so gentle.

They are so like each other, Lesley thought again. The man and the boy—the two dark heads and lean brown faces, Colin's still with the chubbiness of childhood.

And slowly, with complete certainty, she realised that she loved this man, and she loved these children, and she wanted to spend the rest of her life with them.

It was so clear, so sure—this realisation—that she wondered how she could have taken so long to see and to accept.

There wasn't any package deal about it. She wasn't accepting the children because she loved Matt, and she wasn't accepting Matt because of the children.

It was so much simpler than that, so very simple.

Matt turned round then, and saw her.

'Colin's asleep,' he said.

'So is Sarah,' Lesley told him.

'So should you be,' Matt said firmly. 'I'm taking you across right now.'

I'll tell him, Lesley thought with a slow and rising happiness. I'll tell him now when we go out into the warm night.

But as Matt opened the door, one of the nurse-aides came hurrying along the path.

'Sister says could you come and look at one of her patients. He is sick and with fever,' she said breathlessly.

'Probably too much excitement tonight,' Matt said. 'All right, I'll come.'

It doesn't matter, Lesley told herself as she and Matt parted at the hospital entrance, and it didn't.

She could wait—for the right time and the right way to tell Matt that she loved him.

The next day, as soon as her stitches were taken out—by David, because Matt had been called urgently to one of his TB patients—Lesley went to her own ward, feeling very strange to see the bustling activity and not to be part of it.

Peggy Thorpe was in charge, and she told Lesley that her friend was to arrive in Umtata that day.

'Ken and Sylvia will meet her and bring her through,' she said. 'it saves anyone having to make a special journey.' She looked around her. 'This will be quite a change for Mary,' she commented cheerfully. 'Come and inspect our new arrivals, Lesley. Did you hear we'd had twins?'

'I did,' Lesley replied. 'I don't know whether I feel envious or relieved!'

'Beautiful delivery,' the older nurse told her. 'Popped out like peas in a pod, they did, and that's what they look like.'

The two tiny babies lay in a crib beside their proud mother.

'What are their names?' Lesly asked.

'I call them after the two doctors,' the mother told her. 'Dr Matt he deliver this boy, and Dr David he deliver this one—so that is their names.'

'Matt and David—I'm sure the doctors are both delighted,' Lesley said.

It was almost Anna-Marie's lunchtime, and she had promised to help Lesley make candles for the children. Anna-Marie had arranged to do this in Sylvia's kitchen.

'This is where Julie and I made our candles last Christmas,' she said. 'We need the cooker for melting the wax, and we need to have the sink handy, and Sylvia found the old pieces of dinner candle we didn't need. Not terribly exciting moulds, but they're different.'

A blue owl for Sarah, they decided, a pink pig for Colin and a green cat for Jenny.

'Thanks so much, Anna-Marie,' Lesley said when they had finished. 'We leave them in the moulds? I can collect them tomorrow from Sylvia.'

There was no chance that night for her to talk to Matt because he was called over to the hospital, but she didn't mind. As she was walking back to her room she saw Ken unpacking the Land Rover.

'I've just handed our relief nurse over to Peggy—she'll look after her,' he said. 'Oh—Sylvia said this parcel is for you and Matt.'

He handed her a large plastic bag.

'How did Sylvia's check-up go?' Lesley asked.

'Dr Lund seemed to be pleased,' Ken said slowly. 'Cautiously pleased, I'd say. But he is prepared to recommend Sylvia going on with the treatment so that's a relief.'

'I'm glad about that, Ken. I'll see Sylvia tomorrow,' Lesley said. 'Thanks so much for getting the stocking things.'

I won't even look at them now, she decided. I'll save them for tomorrow night.

Christmas Eve.

She could sense the children's excitement growing through the day. Even Sarah had fewer moments of sadness than Lesley had been prepared for.

They were all delighted with the little candles when she produced them at bedtime.

'You and Anna-Marie made them?' Sarah said. Gently she touched her little owl. 'I don't really want my owl to melt, Lesley.'

'I'll tell you what,' Lesley said. 'We'll ask Anna-Marie to help us make some more candles, ones you can keep without burning.'

'Now the stockings,' Colin said impatiently.

The stockings for hanging up had been packed in with the Christmas tree ornaments. There was a large pair of blue stockings, and one yellow one.

'They were Daddy's golf socks,' Colin said. 'From long ago, he said.'

'I remember him wearing them,' Matt said, and for a moment there was a stillness and a sadness on his face.

Lesley, about to touch his hand to let him know that

she understood, stopped. Because Sarah reached out and put her hand on her uncle's arm. She didn't say anything, but her eyes held his steadily. And then, slowly, Matt smiled, and Sarah smiled back.

They all went to Jenny's room, and hung the yellow stocking at the end of her bed.

'For Favver Christmas,' Jenny said. 'Favver Christmas bring toys.'

'We hope so,' Matt agreed. 'Goodnight, little one.'

He put the light out so that there was only the glow of the candle.

'He'll see with that,' Colin said, satisfied. 'Now mine.'

It was when they had lit Colin's candle that Matt thought of something.

'What does Father Christmas do with the special presents?' he asked casually. 'The ones you wrote about in your letters? Because they might be too big for the stockings.'

'He puts them under the tree,' Sarah told them, 'and we wait for them—we open our stockings first.' She looked at Lesley. 'I'm glad you're staying here tonight, Lesley,' she said earnestly. 'We wake quite early, you know, and we take our stockings—'

She stopped, and looked from Matt to Lesley. They had thought of this, and had worked out what would happen.

'As soon as you wake,' Matt said, 'bring your stockings in to my room—that's if there's anything in them, of course—and then wake Lesley in the little spare room. Bring her to my room, and we'll all be together for the stockings. All right?'

'All right,' Sarah said, and the cloud left her brown eyes.

When all three rooms were in darkness, except for the glow of the small candles, Matt and Lesley waited to make sure the children were asleep before Matt crept in and brought out the stockings. Lesley had brought the things Sylvia had bought and had hidden the bag in the cupboard in the small spare room.

They took out the toys and spread them out, Lesley insisting that she was able to sit down on the floor now she'd had her stitches out.

'Sylvia's done marvellously,' Matt said, studying the small, cheap toys. Marbles, balloons, tiny plastic dolls, plastic soldiers, an Indian feather headdress, hairclasps and an Alice band—obviously for Sarah—little plastic capsules to melt in the bath, miniature bouncy balls, a tiny fluffy snowman for Jenny.

'And we put an orange and a silver coin in the toe of each stocking,' Matt said. 'That's what happened for Peter and me. I'm sure he would do the same.'

It took some time before the three stockings were finished and carried back to the children's rooms. While Matt did that Lesley made coffee for them and carried it out to the stoep.

As she handed Matt his coffee the clock inside the hall chimed.

Midnight.

And Lesley knew that this was the right time, and the right place, for her to tell Matt.

She put down her own mug of coffee, and sat down beside him on the swing seat.

'Merry Christmas, Doctor dear,' she said softly.

And she kissed him.

CHAPTER ELEVEN

TER—much later, Lesley realised, bemused—Matt's
s left hers reluctantly, but his arms still held her
se to him.

'Are you saying what I think you're saying?' he
ed, and his dark eyes held hers.

Lesley looked back at him, her own eyes steady.

'I don't know why it took me so long to see,' she
d. 'I love you, Matt, and I love the children, and I
nt us to spend the rest of our lives together.'

His lips found hers again, and his kiss was warm and
w and deep.

And then, determinedly, he released her.

'You're making things very difficult for me,' he said,
t quite steadily, and she could feel the thud of his
artbeat against her body. 'I'm trying damned hard to
member that you're still on the convalescent list.'

'I don't feel convalescent,' Lesley murmured, and
 moved closer to him.

'I gather that,' Matt returned, and there was warm
ughter in his voice. 'But there are guidelines about
s sort of thing, and since I'm your doctor I have to
y by the rules. So—will you please move away, and
p me to do that?'

Lesley moved back into her own corner of the
ing seat.

'Next week?' she asked him.

'Probably,' Matt said cautiously, and the warm laugh-
 was still there in his eyes. He stood up and took
th her hands in his.

'Time for bed,' he said. 'I just know we're going to
 woken very early.'

He was right. It was just after six when Lesley

surfaced through an urgent repetition of her name. She opened her eyes, and looked right into Colin's small freckled face.

'She's waked,' he said triumphantly. 'Sarah, have you got Uncle Matt waked?'

'Yes, she has,' Matt said from the door, running his hand through his dark, sleep-rumpled hair. He lifted Lesley's thin cotton dressing-gown from the end of the bed and looked at it. 'I suppose you'll be decent enough in this to come to my room?'

'With all these chaperones? Of course I will,' Lesley assured him.

Sarah and Jenny were already sitting on Matt's bed, bulging stockings beside them. Matt piled the pillows up, and he and Lesley sat at the top end of the bed with just enough room left for Colin and his stocking.

Jenny put her chubby little hand into her stocking, and drew out a small plastic doll.

'Baby,' she said happily. 'Jenny's baby.'

There was a loud piercing whistle as Colin discovered a bright red hooter. Murray, with an aggrieved look, hid under the bed.

'Oh, it's lovely!'

Sarah, with a blue velvet hairband.

After that the stockings were emptied by all three children—Jenny with wonder and disbelief, Colin with incredible speed and Sarah carefully, each item taken out and inspected before she went on to the next.

'Look, an orange and money,' Colin said, reaching the toe of his stocking first. 'Just like—'

For a moment his voice faltered, and he turned to Matt, dark eyes meeting dark eyes.

'Just like always,' Matt said steadily. 'Your daddy and I had an orange and money in our Christmas stockings, too.'

Colin managed to smile, and the shadows left his eyes.

'Now we look under the tree,' he said. 'To see if
's brought us anything else.'

Sarah, her stocking toys neatly piled up, said confi-
ntially, 'Last year Colin called Father Christmas That
an Christmas. Anything he wanted he used to say,
'll just ask That Man Christmas for it."'

Colin's small freckled face was crimson.

'I was just saying it to be funny,' he said. 'I did know
should be Father Christmas. I did, Sarah.'

'Of course you did,' Lesley said hastily. 'Listen, do
u think we could wait to look under the tree until I
ake coffee for Matt and me?'

'A great idea,' Matt agreed.

Colin stood beside them in the kitchen, jumping with
patience, as they waited for the kettle to boil. When
e two mugs of coffee and three mugs of milk were
a tray he heaved a sigh of relief.

'Now can we go?' he asked. 'Can I open the door?'

There were three gasps when the door was opened,
d they could see the parcels under the tree.

'Which one says "Colin"?' Colin asked. 'Tell me, I
n't wait to read it myself.'

'That one,' Sarah told him, and she handed one parcel
Jenny and then lifted the third one herself. Her eyes,
she felt the parcel, and the pink in her cheeks showed
r excitement, although she was silent.

Colin tore open the paper on his parcel.

'It's the right tractor,' he shouted, 'the one what has
trailer and a fork-lift! He knew I meant this one! Now
u, Sarah.'

Sarah shook her head.

'Jenny next,' she said firmly. 'Look, Jenny, this is
r you from Father Christmas.'

Jenny's present was inside a box, and both Sarah and
lin helped her to open it. At last, wonderingly, the
tle girl held up the fluffy golden dog.

'My doggy?' she asked.

'Your doggy,' Matt assured her. 'Want to see him do his tricks, Jenny?'

He set the toy down on the wooden floor, and turned the key. The little dog turned his somersaults, moved across the floor, somersaulted again and made his way back. Jenny clapped her hands.

'Again!' she ordered, and the dog went through his tricks again, this time watched narrowly by Murray who looked as if he was getting ready to pounce on this strange little intruder.

'No, Murray,' Matt said sternly, and Murray wagged his tail, apologising for even the thought.

'Let's give the dog a rest now, Jenny,' Matt suggested.

Sarah opened her parcel carefully, her small face intent. Lesley, watching her, hoped so much that she wouldn't be disappointed.

'Oh—my bride doll! She's beautiful!'

Sarah's face was alight. Gently she touched the dress, and the veil, and the circlet of pearls holding it in place. At the last minute Lesley had made a tiny bouquet for her, and Sarah touched it wonderingly.

'I've always wanted a bride doll,' she whispered 'And she's exactly what I wanted.'

'Father Christmas always knows, of course,' Colin pointed out.

'Yes, he does,' Sarah agreed.

For a moment, a shared moment, her eyes met Lesley's.

She knows, Lesley thought, but of course she won't say. She'll let Colin and Jenny go on believing until they're old enough to know.

She smiled.

'Can I have a look at her, Sarah?' she asked.

Sarah's brown eyes danced as she handed the doll to Lesley.

'Father Christmas must have got someone very cleve

to make her clothes, don't you think, Lesley?' she said demurely, and Lesley agreed.

After that the children opened their parcels from their grandparents, and Matt took photos of them doing this to send to Clare's mother and father.

'Granny always sends us pretty dresses,' Sarah said with satisfaction. 'And nice bath stuff, too, for Jenny and me.'

Colin looked at his cotton shirt and shorts politely and then, in the pocket, he found a small parcel.

'A Ferrari,' he said, opening it. 'Granddad knows I need a Ferrari. He likes them too.' He turned to Sarah and, in a very audible whisper, said, 'Can we give our presents now, Sarah?'

When Sarah nodded he lifted a parcel from under the tree, and he and Sarah gave it to Matt. It was the bookends they had told Lesley about.

'We started making them for Daddy,' Sarah explained when Colin was suddenly overcome by shyness. 'We wanted you to have them, Uncle Matt. Ken and Sylvia helped us. Colin did the wooden bits, and I did the painting.'

Matt's lean brown face was still.

'I've never had such nice bookends,' he said quietly. 'And I really need them—those books beside my bed are very untidy. Thank you all very much.'

He kissed the three children, holding each one of them tight.

Then there was a present for Lesley, a wooden box with paintings of flowers on it.

'To hold tissues,' Colin told her. 'It's much nicer than just a cardboard box.'

'Of course it is,' Lesley agreed, touched and surprised, and she thanked the children and hugged them too.

Matt drew another parcel from under the tree, and handed it to Lesley. It was a woven scarf, in the lovely bluey-green shades she was so fond of.

'You have to kiss Uncle Matt when you thank him,' Sarah said, and Lesley's heart lifted at the teasing in the little girl's voice.

'Thank you very much, Matt. It's lovely,' she said demurely, and she kissed him and handed him a parcel, glad that she had thought of this as she was leaving Heathrow.

'The new P.D. James,' Matt said, delighted. 'It will be the first book between my bookends! Now I kiss you.'

Colin looked at them. 'I think that's enough kissing,' he said. 'Can we have breakfast now?'

Matt looked at Lesley—a question asked and answered.

'Yes, in a minute,' he said. 'Before we do, though, there's something Lesley and I want to tell you.'

He took Lesley's hand in his.

'Lesley and I are going to be married,' he said.

For some reason, the news didn't seem to surprise the children.

'Good,' Colin said matter-of-factly. 'Now Lesley won't have to go home at night. She can stay here all the time, can't she? And will people call you Mrs Doctor, Lesley, like they called Mummy?'

'Yes, Lesley will stay here,' Matt replied. 'And—I guess they probably will call her Mrs Doctor. Will you mind that, Lesley?'

'Not at all,' Lesley assured him.

'When you get married,' Sarah said seriously, 'will you wear a proper bride dress, like my bride doll?'

'I haven't thought that far,' Lesley told her truthfully. Then she realised what was behind the question.

'Whatever I wear, Sarah, I'd want to have a flower-girl. Two flower-girls, actually. You and Jenny. It might be a quiet wedding, but I would certainly want that. Would you like that?'

Sarah's cheeks were pink.

'Oh, yes, Lesley, and I would see that Jenny behaves. She would be very good, wouldn't you, Jenny?'

Jenny nodded.

'I be good,' she said.

Lesley hugged her.

'I think you'll both be lovely flower-girls,' she said.

'And what I think,' Matt said, 'is let's get on with Christmas Day before we think about weddings. We've got the Christmas party soon.'

The Christmas party, for all the mission staff, was held in the hospital dining-room so that as many of the hospital staff as possible could be there, and yet be on the spot if they were needed.

'And what do you bet,' Matt said as he and Lesley washed up the breakfast dishes, 'that someone will come in needing stitches, or burns dressed, or Mrs Malunga—she's ten days late now—will decide to deliver?'

'You don't sound as if you mind too much,' Lesley told him.

'I don't,' Matt admitted. 'Funny, that, when I used to feel pretty strongly about being on call in London. I don't know what's so different here.'

Lesley stood on tiptoe and kissed him.

'You're different, that's what,' she told him.

'Are you two always going to be kissing?' Colin asked from the doorway.

'Probably,' Matt told him cheerfully. 'Can I give you a hand with the buttons of that shirt?'

Colin looked down at his small chest in the bright cotton short-sleeved shirt his grandparents had sent him.

'There's one button too many,' he said, 'With no hole for it.'

'Not if you match them properly,' Matt told him, and he buttoned the shirt for Colin.

'I'll get Jenny dressed,' Lesley said, but when she went through she found that Sarah, already in her own

Christmas dress, had almost finished putting Jenny's on her.

'I'll put Jenny's shoes and socks on,' Sarah said. 'You'd better get ready, Lesley, it's almost time.'

In the small spare room Lesley hurriedly put on the turquoise cotton dress she had been keeping for today and brushed her hair, leaving it loose on her shoulders. The silver earrings and the necklace her folks had sent were just right with the scooped neck of the dress.

They walked across the dusty compound in the fierce heat, Sarah walking demurely with her bride doll, Colin skipping ahead and Jenny trying to skip as well as her chubby little legs would let her.

The dining-room had been decorated, and there were bright paper chains and lanterns, giving it a very festive look.

'We get presents before we have food,' Colin told them as they found seats. 'Look, Sarah, there's Winston and Sipho.'

The three children ran across the room to meet their friends, and Lesley turned to speak to Anna-Marie, who was sitting behind them.

'I'm on duty, but none of us wear uniform on Christmas Day,' the dark-haired sister told her when Lesley admired her brightly patterned silky dress. 'You look much better, Lesley.'

'I feel a fraud,' Lesley admitted, 'not being back at work because I feel perfectly well.'

'Quite apart from the operation, there's the effects of the anaesthetic—you should know that,' Anna-Marie said. She smiled. 'Anyway, you have to obey doctor's orders.'

She looked across the room at Sarah, showing her bride doll to some friends.

'Looks as if the doll is a success,' she said, and Lesley assured her that it certainly was.

Matt was at the other side of the room, talking to

Sylvia. At a signal from her he clapped his hands, and the crowded room fell silent.

'I don't know if anyone heard anything,' he said, 'but Sylvia and I did. Sounded like bells, we thought. Let's open the door and see if anyone is there.'

He opened the door and a scarlet-suited, white-bearded figure came in, a sack over his shoulder.

'Ho, ho, ho,' he boomed, and all the children laughed and clapped their hands.

'I hear you've all been such good children that you deserve something nice,' he said then. 'Let's see what we have here.'

He opened his sack and took out brightly wrapped parcels, each one with a child's name on it. Small cars and aeroplanes for the boys, bubble bath in Pocahontas containers for the girls.

'Have to go now, kids. My reindeer are waiting and we have a lot to do today. See you next year!'

The children waved as he lifted his empty sack and went out. Colin brought his aeroplane to show Lesley and Matt.

'It's a Concorde,' he said. 'See the shape of its snout?' He leaned forward. 'That wasn't really Father Christmas,' he told them confidentially. 'It's acksherly Ken. He thinks we don't know, but everyone knows. See, in a minute he'll come in in his own clothes and he'll ask us if he's missed Father Christmas.'

That was just what did happen, and Lesley loved it when the children crowded round Ken and told him that, yes, he had missed Father Christmas again.

'He's just been,' one of the older boys said solemnly. 'Didn't you bump into him outside, or see the reindeer?'

'Not a thing,' Ken assured him. 'He must have gone off very quickly. Maybe I'll see him next year.'

Then it was time for the Christmas dinner, and Lesley was surprised and impressed by what the kitchen staff had done for all these people. Turkey, stuffing, small chipolatas—even Brussels sprouts.

'Frozen, of course,' Sylvia said when Lesley commented on it. She looked around and smiled. 'And not enjoyed by many of the children. Just as well we had sweetcorn as well!'

'It was a wonderful Christmas dinner,' Lesley said, when the trifle and the Christmas pudding had been served and she and Sylvia were pouring coffee and tea.

'The Rotary Club which Clare's father belongs to always sends us a donation especially for our Christmas dinner,' Sylvia explained. 'Otherwise we couldn't have anything as special as this.'

She looked around.

'Matt and Anna-Marie off to do some stitching, and Peggy checking on Mrs Mogali,' she said. 'Par for the course. I remember last year Peter and Clare missed out on the meal completely. We had to heat it up for them later.'

For a moment her hand covered Lesley's.

'You've done a good job with the children, Lesley,' she said quietly. 'You and Matt have helped them over this whole thing. We were so worried about them, Ken and I, but we knew that we couldn't take them because of me. We couldn't let them face the possibility of another loss.'

She was quiet for a moment, and then she smiled.

'I'm not asking questions but, well, I couldn't help noticing the way you and Matt look at each other. Yes, I *am* asking questions, I might as well be honest! How are things between the two of you?'

'Things are very good,' Lesley told her. She hesitated, but only for a moment. 'We're going to be married, Sylvia. We only decided last night so we haven't thought about anything more—except that Sarah and Jenny are going to be flower-girls!'

'I'm so pleased,' Sylvia said, not quite steadily. 'I've thought more and more how right you are together, but you had to see it for yourself.' She smiled. 'I'm not promising to dance at your wedding, but if you have it at Thabanvaba I'll certainly be here to wish you well.'

She does look better, Lesley thought. Not well, but better.

'Is that a promise?' she asked.

'It's a promise,' Sylvia replied. Her eyes were steady.

Some of the smaller children had fallen asleep. Matt came through from the hospital and lifted Jenny up, her fair, curly head against the white coat he had donned over his shirt.

'Time we went home?' he asked, and Lesley nodded.

Patience was spending the day with her family so Lesley changed the sleepy little girl into her pyjamas, and put her into her small bed.

'She hasn't had any supper,' Colin said, but Matt said that he didn't think it mattered for once.

'What about you two?' Lesley asked. 'Are you hungry?'

Sarah accepted a slice of toast with Marmite, and Colin thought he could manage some Choc-Pops. By the time they had finished both pairs of dark eyes were drooping.

'I want my tractor right beside me,' Colin said sleepily, and Matt positioned the tractor with its trailer and its forklift at the side of the small boy's bed.

'Goodnight, Colin,' he said, softly, and he bent and kissed the dark head.

'Goodnight, Colin,' Lesley said, and she did the same.

'You know what, Uncle Matt?' Colin said sleepily, and he opened his heavy eyes. 'It was a nice Christmas, wasn't it? I did sometimes miss Mummy and Daddy, but it was still a nice Christmas.'

'Yes, it was,' Matt agreed, and for a moment his voice was less than steady.

Sarah was sitting up in bed, and she made no attempt to hide her tear-streaked cheeks.

'You said it's all right to cry, Lesley,' she said, and

Lesley sat down on the bed beside her and put her arms around the little girl.

'Yes, it's all right to cry,' she said, and she held Sarah close.

Sarah was silent for a little while.

'I'll always miss Mummy and Daddy,' she said. 'Won't I?'

'Yes, you will,' Lesley replied. 'But I think that more and more you'll think of the happy times you had, and that will help the hurting and the missing. And we'll be here, Uncle Matt and I, to do our best to help.'

Sarah nodded.

'It does help,' she said seriously. With a little difficulty, she managed to smile. 'See how nice my bride doll looks, sitting on the bookcase. It's going to be lovely being a flower-girl. I'm looking forward to that.'

'So am I,' Lesley assured her. 'Goodnight, Sarah.'

They kissed her and went out, meeting Murray at the door.

'He seems to know where he's needed most,' Matt said, as the dog padded over and lay down at the side of Sarah's bed. 'What do you bet he'll be up beside her any minute?'

They went outside to the swing seat on the stoep, and sat down in the warm darkness.

'There were some difficult moments,' Matt said after a while. 'But Colin is right—it was a nice Christmas.'

His arm was around her, and he turned his head and kissed her.

'We have some talking to do, you know,' he murmured after a while.

'I know,' Lesley replied. 'But we've got plenty of time, Matt.'

There was warm laughter in his voice.

'I don't know about that, with flower-girls probably already planning their dresses,' he said. He looked at her. 'Lesley, I do want us to be married as soon as possible.'

'So do I, Matt,' Lesley replied. 'My folks will come out, I'm sure, and we could be married here at Thabanvaba. I'd like that.'

'And you can face staying on here, at least for a while?' Matt asked.

'I'd be disappointed not to,' Lesley told him with complete truth. 'Maybe not for the rest of our lives, but there's so much we want to do here, Matt.'

'There's only one other thing,' Matt said, and although his voice was warm and teasing his dark eyes were serious. 'Are we going to feel that three children are enough? No, that isn't fair—asking you that now and expecting you to answer.'

Lesley sat up straight.

'I would want, some time, Matt, to have our child— probably to have two. I don't even need to think about that—I *know*. But how do you feel? Because five is quite a lot of children!'

'Oh, well,' Matt said easily, 'I don't suppose it matters since they outnumber us already anyway.'

He stood up.

'If we sit here much longer we'll both fall asleep,' he said. 'And I'm not forgetting that you're still my patient.'

'Not to mention our professional relationship,' Lesley returned.

'Yes, that, too,' Matt agreed.

In the warm darkness he looked down at her.

'Happy Christmas, Sister Grant,' he said.

And once again, as she had the night before, Lesley said, with all her heart, 'Happy Christmas, Doctor dear.'

WINTER WARMERS

How would you like to win a year's supply of Mills & Boon® books? Well you can and they're FREE! Simply complete the competition below and send it to us by 30th June 1998. The first five correct entries picked after the closing date will each win a year's subscription to the Mills & Boon series of their choice. What could be easier?

THERMAL SOCKS   RAINCOAT   RADIATOR

TIGHTS   WOOLY HAT   CARDIGAN

BLANKET   SCARF   LOG FIRE

WELLINGTONS   GLOVES   JUMPER

T	H	E	R	M	A	L	S	O	C	K	S
I	Q	S	R	E	P	M	U	J	I	N	O
G	A	S	T	I	S	N	O	I	O	E	E
H	T	G	R	A	D	I	A	T	O	R	L
T	A	C	A	R	D	I	G	A	N	A	T
S	H	F	G	O	L	N	Q	S	W	I	E
J	Y	H	J	K	I	Y	R	C	A	N	K
H	L	F	N	L	W	E	T	A	N	C	N
B	O	V	L	O	G	F	I	R	E	O	A
D	O	E	A	D	F	G	J	F	K	A	L
C	W	A	E	G	L	O	V	E	S	T	B

C7L

Please turn over for details of how to enter ⇨

HOW TO ENTER

There is a list of twelve items overleaf all of which are used to keep you warm and dry when it's cold and wet. Each of these items, is hidden somewhere in the grid for you to find. They may appear forwards, backwards or diagonally. As you find each one, draw a line through it. When you have found all twelve, don't forget to fill in the coupon below, pop this page into an envelope and post it today—you don't even need a stamp! Hurry competition ends 30th June 1998.

Mills & Boon Winter Warmers Competition
FREEPOST CN81, Croydon, Surrey, CR9 3WZ
EIRE readers send competition to PO Box 4546, Dublin 24.

Please tick the series you would like to receive
if you are one of the lucky winners

Presents™ ❑ Enchanted™ ❑ Medical Romance™ ❑
Historical Romance™ ❑ Temptation® ❑

Are you a Reader Service™ Subscriber?   Yes ❑   No ❑

Mrs/Ms/Miss/Mr.......................Initials ....
<small>(BLOCK CAPITALS PLEASE)</small>

Surname ....

Address ....

....

....Postcode ....

(I am over 18 years of age)   C7L

One application per household. Competition open to residents of the UK and Ireland only. You may be mailed with offers from other reputable companies as a result of this application. If you would prefer not to receive such offers, please tick box. ❑

Mills & Boon® is a registered trademark of
Harlequin Mills & Boon Limited.